FAKESPEARE

SOMETHING STINKS IN HAMLET

FAKESPEARE

SOMETHING STINKS IN HAMLET

M.E. CASTLE
ILLUSTRATED BY DANIEL JENNEWEIN

{Imprint}
MAKE YOUR MARK

NEW YORK

[Imprint]
MAKE YOUR MARK

A part of Macmillan Children's Publishing Group,
a division of Macmillan Publishing Group, LLC

FAKESPEARE: SOMETHING STINKS IN HAMLET.
Copyright © 2017 Paper Lantern Lit. All rights reserved.
Printed in the United States of America by
LSC Communications, Harrisonburg, Virginia.
For information, address Imprint,
175 Fifth Avenue, New York, N.Y. 10010.

Library of Congress Cataloging-in-Publication Data is available.
ISBN 978-1-250-10159-4 (hardcover)
ISBN 978-1-250-10158-7 (ebook)

Our books may be purchased in bulk for promotional, educational, or
business use. Please contact your local bookseller or the Macmillan
Corporate and Premium Sales Department at (800) 221-7945 ext. 5442
or by e-mail at MacmillanSpecialMarkets@macmillan.com.

Imprint logo designed by Amanda Spielman
Illustrated by Daniel Jennewein

First Edition—2017

10 9 8 7 6 5 4 3 2 1

mackids.com

Who so taketh this, my book,
And doth not ask, their brains shall cook,
Their eyes shall freeze, and bees shall please
To jab and stab their crooked knees.
Where their story after goes,
The Narrator shall then compose.
Beware his prose.

FOR WOODY HOWARD.

Teacher, director, mentor, and friend.
Enjoy your well-deserved retirement.
Just not so much that you won't
come back and work with me again.

FAKESPEARE
SOMETHING STINKS IN HAMLET

DEAR READER,

You are reading this because you expressed interest in the Get Lost Book Club.

Now, I know you might be thinking, *Wait! I never said I was interested in the Get Lost Book Club. I've never even heard of it.* Not to worry. It's my job to pick up on little clues that reveal your interest, like a detective. Maybe it's the number of books on your shelf. Odd things you mutter under your breath or doodle during class. That weird ingredient you insist on putting on your ham sandwiches. You know the one. These signs may seem tiny to you, but you may as well have chiseled an application letter into my front door.

I should warn you, the Get Lost Book Club isn't for the faint of heart. Or the faint of brain.

We believe that the greatest power of a story is its ability to make the world around you disappear for a while . . . and sometimes that "while" can be longer than you expected.

Intrigued? Worried? Downright terrified? You should be. Danger stalks these pages. Also, moat serpents. Sword fights. Poisoned wine. Bad smells. *Really* bad smells.

Do you have what it takes to be a literary adventurer? *I* think you do. But it's up to you to prove it.

If, on the other hand, you want to turn back now, then no hard feelings. I'll understand. Some people just aren't cut out for thrilling chases, fascinating characters, devious villains, and a whole lot of fun.

But if you're ready for an adventure, step right up and follow me. It's time to get lost.

Go on, turn the page. I dare you.

Sincerely,

The Narrator

CHAPTER ONE
THE DAY THAT COULDN'T GET ANY WORSE—SO IT GOT BADDER INSTEAD

"Ready for the serve?"

"Yeth!"

"Do you know what a serve is?"

"Yeth!"

"Are you a neon-green horse?"

"Yeth!"

Kyle Word sighed and hit the Ping-Pong ball across the table. It bounced twice.

Once against his little brother Gross Gabe's side of the table . . .

. . . and once against Gross Gabe's forehead.

"Zoopaloop!" Gross Gabe said, teetering on his hands and knees. "Werb!!"

He hadn't really caught on to the whole speaking thing yet.

"Guess I've seen worse Ping-Pong from an almost-two-year-old," Kyle said, dropping his paddle.

His little brother had woken him up early that

green earwax

swampy morning breath

unknown stains

GUM

smelly diaper

morning. In the middle of a dream about a city made of ice cream. He'd climbed up and said, "Yaaah!" right in Kyle's face, giving him a blast of swampy morning breath that reminded Kyle why he called his younger brother Gross Gabe.

And that was the *high* point of the day.

Because he'd been woken up early, Kyle fell asleep in class only to be woken up (again!) by tiny wet feet. Someone had slipped Roger, the class's pet turtle, down his back.

Later in that very same class, Ms. Mackle saw the sketch he'd drawn of her with fins and fishy eyes labeled *Ms. Mackerel*. She flipped out. He'd thought the fact that he'd drawn her with a whole undersea rock band called Ms. Mackerel and the Mack Attack would've cheered her up. Instead, he had to write a whole page about why drawing people with crazy fish eyes was rude.

A *page*! Full of *words*!

If Kyle had liked words, he wouldn't have been drawing so much in the first place. Pictures were easy. They showed you what they wanted to say right away. Words were like little mazes, full of bends and angles and twists. You had to navigate through them to get what they were saying.

Or Kyle did, at least. It seemed like everyone else had them pretty well figured out.

The day had finally seemed to hit a good point right at the end, when the substitute teacher had put on a movie (something about gorillas). There was just enough glow from the screen that he and his best friend, Becca Deed, were able to sneak some time to work on their comic book series: *The Astounding Adventures of Mal & Cal Worthy.*

Mal and Cal Worthy were dimension-hopping explorers and agents of justice, stopping crime in its tracks across multiple galaxies and times. When Cal worked with his sister, Mal, they were unstoppable. In fact, Kyle believed that the only people who worked better together than Mal and Cal were their creators: Kyle and Becca themselves.

Becca loved words but couldn't draw

anything except for a cartoon cat. Kyle would rather handle a leaky bucket of scorpion venom than a bunch of words. She was the words girl and he was the pictures guy; together, they made the perfect comic book team.

But right as Kyle was finishing one of his best sketches ever, a classmate got up to go to the bathroom with his thermos, tripped over a backpack in the dark, and spilled all his orange-smelling tea on Kyle's sketchbook. Who carried a whole thermos of tea to the bathroom? Who *drank* tea in fifth grade?

And *then* the school bus home got stuck in traffic for an hour. He and Becca had tried to work, but he fell asleep . . . only to wake when someone poured itching powder down his new shirt.

The bus was so late that he'd barely walked

in the door when Mom made him play Ping-
Pong with his baby brother in the basement.
Gross Gabe could be entertained for hours by a
clump of dirt, so Kyle didn't see why he had to
be a babysitter.

Mom hadn't been impressed with his
proposal. "It's your responsibility as a big
brother to make sure Gabe stays safe," she'd said.
"Make sure he doesn't do anything dangerous."

But all Kyle wanted was to go to his room
and sit down with the latest issue of *Mal & Cal
Worthy.* It was the most important one they had
ever done.

He and Becca had already registered and
received the guidelines for the Storyland Young
Storyteller Contest. Any story could be submitted,
including a comic book. If they won, they'd get
a free trip to Storyland in Hawaii.

Becca had finished the script a week ago, and Kyle wanted to put the final touches on the drawings tonight. It was the last chance he'd have, because the deadline to mail the submission was tomorrow. He'd get his weekly allowance tonight, and then he and Becca would send the comic book and entry fee first thing in the morning.

One wouldn't expect a book-themed amusement park to interest Kyle, but books weren't really a theme as much as a flimsy excuse for rides and roller coasters. It was hard to imagine any serious literary thought was behind the Mark Twain Shark Train. Besides, for all his drawings of sleek spacecraft and hyperdrive jets, he'd never actually been in an airplane before. He wanted a real adventure, like Mal and Cal had.

He also wanted to get right back to work on the illustrations, but his mother had said he must watch his brother . . . or else no dessert.

Kyle loved dessert.

Gross Gabe grabbed the Ping-Pong ball and tried to take a bite out of it. His teeth bounced off, which only increased his interest. He went for a second chomp, and Kyle swatted it out of his hand.

"No," Kyle said, speaking clearly and slowly. "Not. Food."

"Foof?" Gross Gabe said, following the ball with his eyes as it sailed away.

"*Not* food," Kyle said.

"Foof," Gross Gabe said, nodding in agreement.

"I really should see if Mom kept the receipt for you," Kyle said, hoisting Gross Gabe off the

Ping-Pong table and setting him down on the carpet. "Maybe we could trade you in for that new game *Blue Blaster Blam 3* or something."

"Bloo!" Gross Gabe said, pointing at the green carpet.

"Yep." Kyle sighed. "Exactly." He went to pick up the Ping-Pong ball and saw it had bounced next to a comic that had slid under the couch. Pulling it out, he realized it wasn't his. It was volume one of *Rachel Never, Hero of No Time*, which Becca had checked out of the public library to help them with the contest.

"Have to make sure I get this to her," Kyle said to himself. He glanced over at Gross Gabe. "And that my brother doesn't eat it first."

"How are you boys doing?" Mom said, coming down the basement stairs in her work apron. She owned a coffee shop and baked all the pastries herself. She was half covered in flour—which was half as covered as she usually was.

"Great," Kyle said. He glanced at the wall clock over his mom's shoulder, and the library book dropped out of his hand, forgotten. "I've only got five minutes till *Allosaurus, MD!*"

He took off past her up the stairs. His favorite show in the entire world was about a dinosaur that had been frozen until the present day and was now a famous brain surgeon. His struggle to fit into modern society was mixed with various medical emergencies and puzzles.

"Well, I hope Halley likes it, too," his mom called up after him as he hit the first floor. "She'll be over in a few minutes."

"WHAT?" Kyle froze in his tracks, his hair swaying back and forth in front of his eyes like upside-down windshield wipers.

"Her mom just called. She and Halley's dad are both coming home from work late, and she asked us to keep an eye on her."

"Couldn't she go somewhere else? Like, anywhere? On earth? Other than here?"

"I guess not, sweetie," she said. "Come here, Gabey! Mommy's gonna scoop you up! Whee!"

Kyle trudged into the kitchen, trying to block out the sound of his brother's squealing in the basement. He opened the fridge and reached into his hiding spot. Waaaaaay in the back, behind the tartar sauce. Nobody ever used tartar sauce, but no one would throw it out, either, and that spot was as safe as Cal Worthy's dimension-hopping skull implant.

In a small Tupperware container was a four-layer beauty of marshmallow, chocolate chips, peppermint bark, and whole Oreos he'd prepared himself. Enough sugar to make any fifth grader do a happy dance all over the place.

But Kyle wasn't dancing.

He was angry. He opened the container and stabbed a spoon into his gooey treat. But even the rush of sugary goodness didn't calm him down. Just *thinking* her name made him grit his teeth.

Halley Pierce-Blossom.

Kyle wasn't sure what was worse: how much she acted like a know-it-all, or the chance that she actually might know it all. She was really smart. *Too* smart.

She brought books to school sometimes.
Not schoolbooks, but books she read just for
fun! What other school stuff did she do for
fun? Pencil-sharpening contests? Gym-locker-
number guessing games?

Becca read, too, *and* she was smart. But she
didn't run around telling everybody how smart
she was all the time. And her voice didn't make
Kyle want to dig his ears out with a soupspoon.
He sighed, carrying his glorious chocreation
from the kitchen into the living room.

"Kyle," he said in a squeaky girl voice as he sat
down on the couch with his snacksterpiece, "did
you know the Andean condor has a wingspan
of up to ten and a half feet? That's 3.2 meters,
of couuuurrrrse." Ugh. The last thing he wanted
was to hang out with Halley the know-it-all.

If only he were actually Cal Worthy, he could jump into a black hole and escape.

Maybe Halley would ignore her parents and stay home alone.

Maybe she'd get lost crossing her yard to his front door.

Maybe an Andean condor would swoop down and carry her off with all its 3.2 meters of wing.

The doorbell rang.

Or maybe not.

"THE GREAT BLACK HOLE OPENED, AND IT WAS FAR TOO LATE FOR MAL AND CAL WORTHY TO DO ANYTHING BUT HOPE IT DEPOSITED THEM SOMEWHERE FRIENDLY." —*THE ASTOUNDING ADVENTURES OF MAL & CAL WORTHY,* ISSUE #1. WORDS BY BECCA DEED, ILLUSTRATIONS BY KYLE WORD.

CHAPTER TWO
NOTE TO SELF: WHEN THE DOORBELL RINGS—RUN!

"Kyle, would you get the door?" Mom yelled up from the basement.

"What?" Kyle asked as he jammed his fingers in his ears.

"I said, WOULD YOU GET THE DOOR?"

"Sorry, can't hear you!" Kyle shouted, cranking up the TV as *Allosaurus, MD*'s theme song began to blare.

The doorbell rang again.

That girl just wouldn't give up.

Kyle heard his mom's footsteps on the basement stairs. He quickly slipped the container with his secret TV snacksterpiece under the couch.

"Well, of course you can't hear me with the TV turned up to a billion," Mom said, taking the remote from Kyle's hand while holding Gross Gabe. "Honestly, Kyle. She'll only be here for an hour or two."

She turned the TV down and went to answer the door.

"Yeah," Kyle said, sinking deeper into the couch, "but it'll feel like weeks."

He ignored the sounds of Halley coming into the house for as long as he could. Then he felt the couch sink as she sat down next to him. She plunked her backpack at her feet. It was covered in glittering pink starfish stickers. Where did you even *buy* glittering pink starfish stickers?

"Hey, Kyle," she said.

He turned to face her the same way he'd turn to face a loaded crossbow.

"Halley," he said.

"What're you watching?" Her deep, dark brown eyes shone. They reminded Kyle of chocolate M&M's. But *that* just reminded him that with her there, he'd never be able to eat his chocreation. Too much risk that his mom might see it, or that Halley might tell on him. Worse yet, that Mom would see it and make him share it.

"*Allosaurus, MD*," Kyle said. He turned back to the TV. "Last episode was a cliff-hanger. He had to perform emergency heart surgery, but

his big dino-hands weren't nimble enough. Now
we see if he can figure it out."

"Hmmm. I don't think I can do my homework

with the TV on," she said. "I need to study for
our spelling test tomorrow."

"Kyle," his mom said, coming into the room
at exactly the wrong moment. "Is it true you
have a spelling test?"

"Depends what you mean by *true . . .* ," Kyle muttered.

"Kyle," she said in a stony voice.

"Yes," Kyle admitted. "But . . . I already know the words really well."

"Great!" Halley said happily. "You can test me!" She flapped the list of words under his nose. "Go ahead!"

Kyle tried to keep one eye on the show as he sounded out a word.

"C . . . con—" The letters seemed to dance in front of him like evil clowns. He blinked and put the rest of the word together. "—skeeyoose."

"What?" Halley said, grabbing the sheet back. "It's not conskeeyoose, Kyle. It's *conscious.* Conskeeyoose isn't a word."

It felt like she'd stabbed him in the forehead with a fountain pen.

"Sounds like you need a little more time to study, yourself," Kyle's mom said to him, with one eyebrow raised. She set Gabe on the couch. "Dad's in the upstairs kitchen. He'll have dinner ready in an hour—that should give you enough time." She clicked off the TV and walked out. Her baking projects had totally conquered the house's real kitchen, so they'd added a little one for meals. Dad, who worked mostly from home, was its proud master. "He's got a big pot of tomato soup going."

"Erch," Kyle said involuntarily, his head twitching. The mention of healthy food tended to get that reaction out of him.

"Erch!" Gabe repeated happily.

Mom frowned. "You should set a better example for Gabe, you know. You're both growing boys—tomatoes are good for you. Besides, you know how sweet Dad makes his soup; you can barely taste them."

"Erch!" Gabe said again.

Mom sighed. "I'll leave you to your studying."

Kyle was so boiling mad, he could practically feel bubbles rising from his scalp. This was a very important episode. His parents might let him use a computer to watch it online tomorrow, but he was sure someone would spoil it for him by then. Cal Worthy would never let someone get in the way of his favorite TV show—and Mal would have his back! Unfortunately, Kyle was short on allies at the moment. The closest around was his brother, and he wasn't going to be writing any speeches on his behalf anytime soon.

"Teeef!" Gross Gabe said, followed by a wall-shaking belch.

"Aww," Halley said, completely unaware that she had just ruined Kyle's life. "C'mere, little guy!" She scooped Gabe up into her arms.

"Don't encourage him," Kyle said.

"Who's the cutest?" Halley went on.

"I'm warning you. You don't understand the smells he's capable of producing."

"*You're* the cutest!" she cooed as Gabe laughed happily.

"Hey," Kyle snapped. "This was your idea. Are we working or not?"

"Just a second," Halley said. "Woocha woocha woo! Who's a little woocha woo?" Kyle felt sick to his stomach. At least he hadn't wasted his chocolate masterpiece—if he had eaten it, it would have all come up halfway through the second *woocha.*

The bell rang again.

"Delivery truck outside!" his mom called from the kitchen. "I'm all floury. Kyle, could—"

"Yes, I could!" Kyle said, speeding away from the stomach-turning scene. He opened the door just in time to see a deliveryman get into his truck and drive off. On the stoop was a strange-looking package. It wasn't in a cardboard box, but a small wooden crate. Kyle thought it might be some new baking supplies for his mom, but as he bent to pick it up, he saw the label:

To: Kyle Word

But Kyle's birthday wasn't for ages—for 249 days, to be exact. So why was he getting a package?

"What is it?" Halley asked, appearing behind him.

"I dunno," Kyle said. He carried it into the living room. Halley trailed after him, carrying Gabe on her hip.

The crate was nailed shut, but after a minute Kyle was able to pry the top off with his fingers. Instead of foam peanuts, it was stuffed with straw—straw that smelled like it had been soaked in liquefied trout for a week.

"Is this from a historical society or something?" Halley said, putting Gabe down. "Are you a Civil War reenactor?"

Kyle ignored her and brushed away the layer of straw. Underneath it were two books, one on top of the other. He picked up the first and squinted as he read the title.

29

"*Hamlet*?" Kyle said. "Is that like a small ham?"

"Ugh," Halley said. "You've never heard of *Hamlet*? It's only maybe the most famous play ever. I mean unless you count the Ancient Greeks, of course . . ."

"This?" Kyle said, looking at the cover. "It looks pretty boring to me. The cover's not even illustrated—it's just brown with one word on it. A word that sounds like a miniature pork product."

The book was solid and heavy. Almost like picking up one of Gross Gabe's full diapers. A piece of paper slipped out from between the pages. Halley snatched it up and read:

"*To the newest member of our society, the Get Lost Book Club.* I'm impressed, Kyle," she said. "I wasn't sure you knew what a book was." She cleared her throat. "*May this be the first of many adventures. Sincerely, the Narrator.* And there's a poem here, too. . . ."

"Give me that!" Kyle said, trying to grab for the paper, but she moved it out of his reach. He sighed, peering over her shoulder instead. The note was written in the sloppiest cursive he'd ever seen, and, just like on the spelling worksheet, the letters seemed to skitter around on the page like insects.

"Ahem . . ." Halley took a deep breath and read:

Listen! A prince of skulls cries in the dark—
Beware, for none see the ghostly mark.
To read or not to read, that is the question,
But first off, you must end
the prince's oppression.
Then flip the final page and reach "The End,"
And soon enough, you will be home again.

"Weird," Kyle said. Halley handed the note to him. He quickly glanced over it again and then let it drop to the floor as he turned to the book.

"You really don't know who sent it?" Halley asked. "Huh. Maybe this was a surprise for you from your parents or something. I'm sure they're embarrassed to have a son in fifth grade who can't read yet."

"I can read!" Kyle said quickly. He almost shot back that Halley couldn't draw, but for all he knew she might be great at that, too.

Halley crossed her arms. "Oh yeah? Prove it."

"Fine!" Kyle flipped through the pages. "Here we go. It starts . . ." He took a very deep breath and forced his eyes to move slowly across the page: "*Act One. Scene One. Eli's nose.* Er . . .

Elvis gnome. Sorry, wait. That's *Elsinore. A platform before the castle. Francisco at his post. Enter Bernardo. BERNARDO: Who's there?"*

The book was so heavy, his hands were starting to shake. How many pages were in this thing? He could barely turn one. . . .

That was when he realized—it wasn't just his hands that were shaking. The *book* was shaking.

He let go. The book hit the ground sooner than it should have. Because it wasn't just shaking. It was *growing.*

Kyle heard some knocking and his mom calling from the kitchen, but her voice was distorted and weirdly distant. He couldn't make out what she was saying.

The book was the size of a dog, a coffee table, a car. The covers started opening

and closing slowly, then a little faster, then
so fast they were a blur. *Chomp! Chomp!*
Chompchompchomp!

"What's happening?" Halley shrieked. Her eyes were as large as softballs.

The book was going to eat them!

Then there was a weird *crackle*, and Kyle felt his ears pop. The room dissolved in a blur as the book flipped open, and suddenly the whole world was swirling printed ink on paper, rushing and rushing around them. . . .

Everything went dark.

CHAPTER THREE
CORRECTION: EVERYTHING STINKS

Kyle blinked slowly. His head hurt.

Man, what a weird dream, he thought. He'd dreamed that Halley had come over, acted like a know-it-all, and ruined his afternoon of TV. And then, as if that weren't bad enough, a book had shown up and swallowed the world.

Well, at least he was awake now. Home in bed, safe and sound.

Kind of.

Maybe.

Certain things, he noticed, were *different*.

Three things, to be precise.

1. He was lying on hard stone. Which
   was definitely not what his bed normally felt like.

2. When he opened his eyes, he saw
   the open sky, which was not what
   he normally saw on his bedroom
   ceiling.

3. He smelled dead rats and rotting
   cabbage, which he was pretty sure
   he hadn't stuffed under his bed.

"Ugh," said a girl's voice.

Kyle sat up. There was Halley, also starting to
sit up, still holding Gross Gabe, who was asleep.

"It wasn't a dream," Kyle said. "It wasn't a

dream. But that means, that means . . ." He looked around at what was clearly the top of a castle tower. "That means I really did miss *Allosaurus, MD*! Noooooo!" he shouted at the overcast sky.

"Kyle?" Halley looked around. Her face was as pale as an overcooked noodle. "What happened? Where are we?" Gabe stirred and twisted in her arms.

"Why are you asking me?" Kyle asked. "All I did was open some book, and now *poof*! Here we are! Why don't *you* tell *me* what's going on? *You're* the one who likes to read!"

"Wooooooo," Gross Gabe shouted, waking up. Halley set him down.

"Well, it kind of looks like . . ." Halley trailed off, then she gasped. "I think we're in a castle. Look at the crenellations!"

"The *what*?" Kyle said.

"The border on the edge of the tower where the stones look like the teeth of a zipper," Halley said, rolling her eyes. "So archers can shoot between them." She paused for a second as her nose scrunched up. "Is somebody boiling muddy boots?"

"I think something is rotten," Kyle said, sniffing again. "It's such a *weird* smell, though. It's not just garbage and dirty

laundry and stuff. It's like somebody stunk up the castle on purpose."

"Maybe," Halley said. "Castles aren't known for their great sanitation, but this is a little much."

She swatted at her nose as if she were trying to bat it off her face. "Maybe something bad happened. A spill or something."

Kyle stood up and peered out over the side of the tower. Where were they? England? Finland? Disneyland?

Oh please, he thought, *let it be Disneyland!* But Kyle had been there last year, and he didn't remember Disneyland smelling like a truck full of tree mulch driving into a tar pit.

"Okay, okay, okay," Halley said, pacing in a tiny circle. "So we're in a castle. Why? Were we just talking about castles?"

Kyle crossed his arms, annoyed. "Halley, I just read to you that Scene One takes place in a castle! It was *your* idea for me to read. The least you could do is pay attention."

But Halley still wasn't listening. She was spinning around wildly, looking in all directions. "Kyle! Do you know what this means? I think . . . I think we're inside the book. I think we're actually *in* the world of *Hamlet*! This must be Elsinore! The royal castle of Denmark a long, long time ago."

Kyle gaped at her. "But I don't want to be in a book!" he said. "I don't even want to be in a book*store*!"

"Stop yelling," Halley snapped. "I'm trying to think." Her forehead wrinkled like an accordion. "Usually I'd just retrace my steps to get home, but we didn't take any steps."

"If you're right, and this is page one of the book, maybe we have to read the last page?" Kyle suggested.

Halley's eyes widened. "Yeah. . . . Reading the beginning got us in here—so maybe reading the ending is the way out. Didn't the poem say something about reaching the end and going home again?"

"I think so," Kyle said. "It makes sense. We jumped through time and space like Mal and Cal Worthy!"

"Who?" she asked.

"Nobody," Kyle said quickly. He had never shown anybody except Becca his sketches of the Worthies, and he wasn't about to show them to a girl whose taste in art involved sparkly starfish.

". . . Well?" Halley said. "What are you waiting for? Read it!"

"I don't have it," Kyle said.

"What do you *mean* you don't have it?" Halley said. Her face had gone from white to ketchup red.

"Don't you remember anything?!" Kyle said, barely containing his frustration. "The book got as big as a house! It tried to eat us!"

"Leave it to you to fail at doing something easy like holding on to a book," Halley said. "I thought *reading* it would be the hard part."

"I read just fine!" Kyle said, getting even angrier. "Obviously, or we wouldn't be here, would we?"

CRACKLE! CRACKLE!

For a moment he thought a thunderstorm had appeared out of nowhere. But when he looked up, the sky was still blue. In fact, it didn't really sound like thunder at all. It sounded like a giant was flipping through a book right over their heads. Kyle gulped as a loud voice began to speak:

```
They had uncovered the secret
of the book, but their journey
to find that book would be
an adventure all its own.
```

Kyle and Halley stared at each other wide-eyed.

The voice sounded like it was coming

through a loudspeaker in the sky, yet . . .
not. It wasn't echoing right. It sounded big
and booming, and strangely close—like it
was coming from inside Kyle's own head. But
Halley's return stare told him she'd heard it,
too.

"Um . . . hello?" Kyle said. They waited a
second.

"Whoever you are, can you help us?" Halley
asked.

Don't mind me; I'm the Narrator.
I just tell the story. You're
the ones who must live it. I
may drop in from time to time
to check on you and give a
hint. Which I just did, if you
were paying attention. Now if

```
you'll excuse me, it seems I
have some business in Verona.
```

The giant-page-flip sound filled the air again.

"Ve-where-a?" Kyle said.

"Beats me," Halley said. "But I was right! The book *is* the way out, which means it must be around here somewhere. This castle must have a hundred rooms. One of them is bound to be a library."

"I don't think it's a good idea to go storming into the castle," Kyle pointed out. "In fact, the whole point of a castle is to keep people from storming it. They'll throw us in the dungeon if we get caught. And if it smells this bad up *here*, just imagine the dungeon's stench."

"Do you have a better idea?" Halley said.

"Yes!" Kyle said. "I think we should find whoever's in charge and beg for mercy. Maybe impress them with our magical future clothes. *Then*, we can work on finding the book. Gross Gabe thinks I'm right. Don't you, Gross G—"

He turned to look at his brother—just in time to see Gross Gabe crawl right off the edge of the tower.

CHAPTER FOUR
BABIES MAY SHIFT DURING FLIGHT

Kyle's stomach dropped as if it had just plunged from a castle wall, too. Kyle and Halley sprinted for the edge of the parapet, and Kyle dived to his belly.

"Zoom!" Gross Gabe shouted. He had fallen all of six feet before his diaper had snagged on a gargoyle. He waved his arms happily, swaying back and forth.

"That's not gonna hold for long," Halley said. "We have to get him!"

Kyle started to shimmy over the edge. He barely fit through the gap in the crenellation. He stretched his arms as far as they went, but still he couldn't quite get his hands around Gabe.

Mom was going to kill Kyle! She'd told him it was his job to make sure Gabe played safely, and even in a Mal and Cal adventure, swinging a hundred feet above ground wouldn't qualify as "safe."

"Hey! You up there!" a man's voice called from below. Looking down past Gabe's butt, Kyle saw two guardsmen in chain mail and helmets, carrying spears. "Where did you come from?!" one of them yelled.

"Help!" Kyle shouted back. Couldn't they see his brother was in danger? "Please, help!"

But they made no move to help. They stayed where they were, leaning on their spears and chewing something that from a distance looked very much like doughnuts.

"Don't make us come up there!" one of them said. But his mouth was full, so it sounded more like *Dumph mumph iss com up furr.*

Kyle's mouth was dry. What would Mal and Cal Worthy do?

"Lower!" he called to Halley. "I need to go lower!"

Halley locked her arms around his ankles, and he eased himself over the edge. His

stomach leaped for a moment as his weight shifted completely off the tower—and his stomach wasn't great to begin with, thanks to the rotten-vegetable-and-moldy-cardboard stink.

"A little lower!" he called again.

"Urrg," she said, straining to hold him. "Just hurry up or you'll be going a *lot* lower." She leaned farther over the edge, and Kyle finally got his hands on Gross Gabe's waist.

"Zoom!" Gross Gabe yelled again, and pushed off the gargoyle with his legs. The momentum made his weight pull much harder on Kyle, and he

heard the gritty sound of
Halley's stupid sparkly
hot-pink sneakers
sliding off the tower. . . .

"Ahhhhh!" Halley
screamed.

"Ahhhhh!" Kyle
screamed.

"Zoooooooom!"
Gross Gabe laughed.

So this is it, Kyle
thought as the world
seemed to slow down. This
was how he would meet
his end. A victim of a giant,
hungry book and gravity.

Well, at least it was
original.

FLOOF!

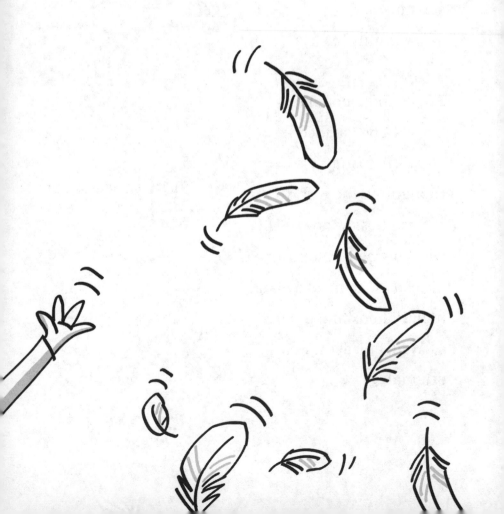

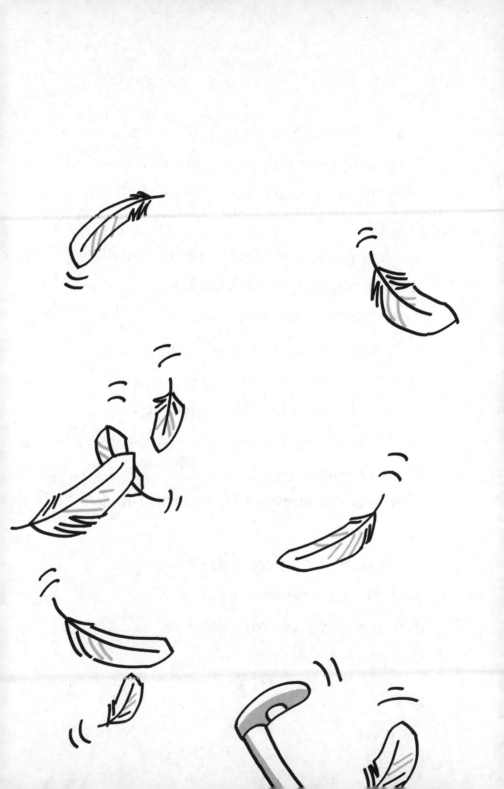

For a second, Kyle thought they must have fallen into the world's largest marshmallow, but marshmallows didn't smell like a crowded duck pond.

He came to the surface, coughing out dirty fluff, and Halley's and his brother's stunned faces emerged a moment later.

"The goose down!" one of the guards shouted, as both of them rushed forward.

"Foo you know how fong it fook to fill tha fart?" The other guard spat out feathers as he spoke. "I mean, cart?"

Kyle pulled himself to his feet, brushing goose feathers from his shirt.

"Yeah, we're, uh, real sorry about that," he said. "But we don't want to be here, either. Our arrival was completely an accident."

"Could you direct us to the library, please?" said Halley. "We're trying to find *Hamlet*."

"They want the prince!" the fatter guard said, tightening his grip on his spear.

"Oh no," the other guard groaned. "Are you one of Prince Hamlet's stupid pranks? You tell him that his crazy jokes are wasting our time!"

Halley shook her head quickly, her ponytail snapping back and forth like the tail of a kite.

"No," she said. "We're not playing any pranks. We're just looking for the library."

"You must be spies, then!" the fat guard said. "I told you, Bernardo."

"Actually, Francisco, you said they were gnomes invading from a flying ship, but as usual I tried to ignore you."

"Gnomes are real, I'm telling you," Francisco

said, bristling. "You just need to pay more attention."

"Attention to what?" said Bernardo. "Your ravings about creatures from fairy land? Like when you started yelling at that horse yesterday?"

"*It was a unicorn!*" snapped Francisco, growing red in the face.

"IT WAS A HORSE WITH A CARROT IN ITS MOUTH!" Bernardo shouted, rounding on Francisco. Kyle turned to Halley.

"This is our chance," he whispered. *"Run!"*

CHAPTER FIVE
HISSSSSSSSSSSSSSSSSSSSSSSSSSSSS

Kyle scooped up Gross Gabe and tore across the courtyard to a small side gate in the castle wall. If only he had Cal Worthy's super jet pack . . . The rapid smack of Halley's footsteps sounded right behind him. If everyone guarding the castle was as distractible as the first pair of guards, maybe they had a chance.

"Hey! Stop!" Francisco shouted.

Chain mail clinked as Francisco and

Bernardo gave chase. Kyle and Halley dashed through the open gate, only to skid to a stop at the edge of a moat—a moat twelve feet wide, filled with pitch-black water, and even if they could swim across it, the opposite side was too steep for them to be able to climb out.

If Kyle remembered anything about castles, there was only one way across the moat.

"Drawbridge is this way!" said Halley, executing a quick right turn. Kyle rolled his eyes as he ran after her. She even interrupted his *thoughts.* "Hurry!"

"I'm . . . hurrying . . . ," he gasped. His brother didn't weigh much more than a potted fern, but carrying him wasn't easy, especially because all the bumping around was making Gross Gabe even more gassy than usual.

"Weee—URP—eeee!" he shouted. "URRRRP!"

They came to a corner. Kyle couldn't see past Halley, so when she stopped suddenly to turn, he had no warning. He plowed right into her.

Once again, all three of them went tumbling through the air.

SPLASH!

Kyle hit the icy water with a painful belly flop. A massive gulp of moat water forced its way into his mouth. It tasted like a ten-year-old truck tire. He pushed his head above water and blinked his eyes clear, shivering, coughing, and spitting.

Kyle grabbed hold of his brother as Halley

popped up right next to them. Her soaked hair was plastered to her face like she'd had a fight with a plate of spaghetti . . . and lost.

Francisco and Bernardo reached the edge of the moat. Then they stopped. Bernardo shook his head with a smirk.

"Maybe you were right," he said. "These people are way too clumsy to be real spies. I bet Prince Hamlet *did* set this up."

"Ugh," Francisco said. "Thank the bard he's only a prince and not the king. Can you imagine how difficult life will be if Prince Hamlet *actually* becomes king?"

"I don't want to imagine it," Bernardo said with a shudder, and Kyle wondered what kind of awful pranks this Prince Hamlet had played to be so disliked.

"Come on," Francisco said, "let's get out of

SOMETHING STINKS IN HAMLET

here. I've got another box of cookies hidden in the guardhouse."

They walked away, their voices getting too faint to hear.

Kyle's face scrunched up in puzzlement as he continued to tread water. Even with a big moat like this, the guards seemed awfully sure they couldn't possibly escape.

```
Foolish as Bernardo and
Francisco could be, they
weren't quite foolish enough to
dive into a snake-filled moat.
```

"A *what*-filled moat?" Halley shouted. "Could you maybe have mentioned that before we jumped in?!"

The only reply was a sound like a slow air leak.

And after a moment, it got much, much louder.

HISSSSSSSSSSSSSSSSSSSSSSSSSSSSSSSS

"SNAKES!" Kyle said. He paddled hard in the opposite direction, tightening his grip on his wriggling brother. Halley splashed feverishly after them. The cold water made his joints ache, and his feet were starting to go numb.

This was worse than when Kyle's class had taken a trip to a lake and Kyle got chased around for an hour by a pack of angry kindergartners he'd tricked into thinking geese spat poison darts.

He made a mental note to add poison-dart-spitting geese to the list of villains Mal and Cal Worthy would fight in his comic.

Both sides of the moat were six feet of smooth stone. Kyle couldn't have climbed that from solid ground, let alone floating with a squirming poop factory under his arm.

But they wouldn't get to the wall anyway.

HISSSSSSSSSSSSSSSSSSSSSSSSSSSSSSSS

More snakes floated at them from that direction.

And the two guards were long gone.

"Fissy?" Gross Gabe said, looking at the snakes.

"Well," Kyle said, "I guess this is it." He was numb past his ankles now. "Halley, I want you to know, I don't really like you. I think you're an annoying know-it-all and I'm not happy that I'll die without finding out what happened to my favorite televised dino . . . but even so, I'd never wish for you to get eaten by moat snakes."

"T-t-thanks, K-kyle," Halley said, her chattering, almost-tap-dancing teeth making her even harder to understand. "I think you're a la-la-lazy, obnoxious s-slacker with n-n-no imagination, but if I could s-s-s-save you from w-w-watery, venomous d-doom, I w-would."

He was a little offended by her *no imagination* remark, before remembering that he'd never shown her or even told her about his comics. He also didn't know what *venomous* meant, but he wasn't about to bring that up at a time like this.

"Sorry, little bro," Kyle said to Gross Gabe, the snakes less than three feet away on all sides. "I would've liked to see you grow up to be more of a person than a fart machine."

"Fissy!" Gross Gabe shouted, waving happily.

KER-PLUNK!

Suddenly, Kyle got hit in the face with another mouthful of mossy moat water. Something white and heavy crashed into the water and then bobbed up. With a unified hiss, the snakes pivoted, moving off in the direction of the splash. Kyle felt a scaly tail whip his ankle and shuddered.

He turned around to see what had saved them.

And saw a human skull floating in the water.

CHAPTER SIX
REAL BOYS AREN'T AFRAID TO WEAR TIGHTS

Kyle gulped. Whose skull *was* that?

"Y-y-you've g-got to b-be kidding me," Halley said, shivering even harder. "How m-much s-s-scarier can this place g-get?"

A lot, actually. Just wait until you get to the part where—

"NOT HELPING!" Kyle bellowed.

```
You're right; spoilers
always make things less
fun. Please, continue.
```

"Pssst!" A whisper came from behind them. "This way! Before the snakes come back for you!"

Kyle and Halley looked around. A door had opened in the side of the moat, halfway up the castle wall. Kyle and Halley swam as fast as they could for it while Gross Gabe made motorboat noises that sounded suspiciously like farts.

Halley pulled herself up onto a small stone landing just inside the open door. Kyle handed Gross Gabe to her before pulling himself up. Whoever had whispered to them had already vanished into the castle through a second door, which was barely cracked open.

Shivering, Kyle advanced down the passage,

Halley and Gross Gabe right behind. Their soggy shoes squished against the stone floor. The doors closed behind them with a SNAP, and Kyle jumped.

At first it was too dark to see anything. Then Kyle made out a dim flicker of orange-yellow candlelight, a palm-size glow that grew brighter as a person came toward them.

The light revealed two things.

First, that the room they were in was full of books, shelved and neat.

Second, the room was also full of skulls.

Great. It was bad enough that they were in a library. Kyle thought about just turning around and taking his chances with the snakes. He'd never liked books much to begin with, but after today he would never trust one again.

The footsteps were getting closer.

"I did not escape a pack of snakes just to be dinner for the world's deadliest librarian," Halley whispered.

"All librarians are

deadly," Kyle whispered, as he and Halley carefully backed up, only to find they had nowhere to go.

"THE BODILESS SKULLS RUSHED AT THEM, AND THEY MET THE CHARGE HEAD-ON. OR HEAD-OFF, AS IT SEEMED." —*THE ASTOUNDING ADVENTURES OF MAL & CAL WORTHY*, ISSUE #3. WORDS BY BECCA DEED, ILLUSTRATIONS BY KYLE WORD.

He looked around for a weapon. Where was Cal Worthy's giant, scorpion-inspired mace when you needed it? The best he could do was grab a thick, heavy book from a nearby stand. It looked to be about a thousand pages. At last one of these things might come in handy.

Following Kyle's lead, Halley put Gross Gabe down and picked up a book of her own. Gross Gabe started chewing the pages of a paperback that he found on the ground.

The figure came around a tall shelf, and Kyle was dazed by the sudden bright candle flame. He blinked at the shadowy image. This was just like what happened in the Mal and Cal Worthy stories. Which was exciting but at the same time, Mal and Cal Worthy had had a lot more training in battling evil skeletons than he had.

"Stay back!" Halley shrieked. "You won't take our skulls, mister!"

"Your skulls?" the shadow echoed. "But I—"

"BOOKS AWAY!" Kyle shouted.

Halley and Kyle threw their books. They missed by several feet. The stranger moved his candle, and he turned out to be a barely four-foot-tall boy, with a much taller shadow.

He flinched and then backpedaled as the books flew overhead, almost tripping over his own feet.

"Wait! Wait!" he called out. The boy seemed to be about Kyle and Halley's age. "I was just trying to help! See? I brought you tea to get the moat taste out of your mouths! It's the worst."

He held out his hands, and Kyle could see he had a candle in one and a pair of short clay mugs in the other.

The boy was also wearing the strangest clothes Kyle had ever seen—even stranger than his great-aunt Susan's floral sundresses with square-dancing cats appliquéd down the front.

He had on a loose shirt with odd puffy sleeves, an embroidered black vest that went past his waist, a hat that looked like a deflated balloon animal on his head, and dark-green tights. *Tights.* It was like the boy's mom shopped at a store where everything was designed by a blind three-toed sloth.

"But . . . but . . . ," Halley said. "The skulls!"

"Oh!" the boy said, looking around. "You

mean these? They're sweet skulls, made of sugar. Spun sugar comes in almost any shape— camel, weasel, whale, whatever you want! I keep them here to distract the snakes, and they seem to like skull-shaped the best. My uncle Claudius put the snakes in the moat to keep people out."

Kyle thought that in Mal and Cal Worthy's next adventure, they should journey to the Amazon and collect a poison snake or two. It could help keep certain pink-sneakered villains out of their secret lair.

Gross Gabe had already abandoned his tasteless book and started gnawing on a skull. He giggled between tiny bites. Kyle wondered if he was actually part puppy, and not just teething like their mother said.

"I'm surprised those bizarre clothes you're wearing didn't sink you," the boy said. "Don't tell me—you're from Verona. I hear the Italians have a very different sense of style—lots of reds and blues. Wouldn't suit me at all."

"And who are you, exactly?" Kyle asked.

The boy cleared his throat. "Sorry, I should introduce myself. Hamlet. I'm the prince. Not that my uncle treats me like it. Not that *anyone at all* has treated me like royalty lately."

"Wow!" Halley said. "Hamlet himself! It's an honor."

"Nice that someone thinks so," Hamlet said glumly. He set the candle down on a table and handed one mug each to Halley and Kyle.

"Prince, huh?" Kyle said suspiciously, eyeing the mug in his hand. He remembered what the guards had said about the prince. "You have a crown?"

"I do . . . somewhere." Hamlet sighed.

"Haven't seen the thing in days. I have a feeling my uncle might've taken it. Not that he needs my little prince crown, since he wears the *king's* crown." There was a little bitterness in that statement. "Hard to say, though. Things have been weird around here."

Shivering, Kyle raised the mug to his lips. The tea was almost too hot to drink. He had never had tea before. Mom drank it with her cookies, but he'd never tasted it. It always kind of looked like dirty bathwater to him. And given that his last tea-based experience had ruined a sketchbook, he was extra-reluctant this time. Still, anything had to be better than tasting the peppered-asphalt-and-boiled-cactus flavor of moat water the rest of the day.

The tea was a little bitter, but it warmed him up nicely. He grabbed a sugar skull and broke off the jaw, then sank it into his mug. Even better.

Once his nose warmed up, he realized that it didn't smell quite so bad in here. Just the musty old smell of books, which— besides making him think about books—wasn't awful.

"Thanks," he said. "I'm Kyle, and this is Halley. The tiny explorer eating your skulls is Gabe."

"Charmed," Hamlet said. "So how *did* you get here? I haven't seen any caravans or wagons in days, and what with the way my uncle has treated travelers lately, I didn't think anybody was even trying to visit anymore."

Uh-oh. That didn't sound good.

"A book was sent to me," Kyle said. "A book with your name on it. I started to read it, and then it became huge

and swallowed us up, and the next thing we knew we were in this castle."

That's a pretty underwhelming way to describe it. Hardly gets into the beauty of the book

```
or the wonder of traveling
between worlds at all.
```

"Forgive us if we're too busy trying not to get swallowed by serpents to think about the art of book traps," Kyle said.

"Agreed," Halley said. "Running for our lives is distracting. Not that you didn't know how much danger we'd be in, of course."

"Gah!" Gabe said.

```
What fun would there be
with no danger? Wouldn't
be much of a story.
```

"We didn't ask to be in a story," Kyle said sourly.

"Who are you talking to?" Hamlet asked.

Halley and Kyle looked at each other.

"You can't hear him?" Kyle asked.

"Hear who?" Hamlet said. He was curious, but he wasn't staring at them like they were out of their minds. "Maybe I was right!"

"Right about what?" Halley asked, forever curious. Kyle was surprised she knew how to ask a question without raising her hand to answer it herself.

"It means I can prove to Uncle Claudius that I'm *not* crazy or an irresponsible prankster!" Hamlet said triumphantly. "I've gotten a reputation as the castle lunatic."

Remembering the guards' conversation, Kyle eyed Hamlet warily. Francisco and Bernardo had seemed pretty sure that Hamlet was up to no good. But if anyone was a prankster in this castle, Kyle would have said it was the Narrator.

"If I ever want to be treated like a prince again," Hamlet continued, "I need to prove that what I saw was real."

As Kyle watched Hamlet hop a spontaneous jig, he

wondered if Hamlet might have celebrated his non-craziness a bit too soon.

"What you saw?" Halley asked. "What did you see?"

Hamlet stopped his dance. His delighted grin flattened into dead seriousness as he leaned forward to whisper, "*The ghost.*"

CHAPTER SEVEN
WHERE THERE'S A GRAVEYARD, THERE'S A . . . GHOST?

The word *ghost* echoed and bounced around the room, sounding just about as scary as . . . well . . . a ghost.

"Psh," Halley said, rolling her eyes. "Ghosts aren't real."

"But books that hurl people through time and space are?" Kyle shot back as Hamlet frowned at her.

"You were just talking to an invisible being that I can't hear," Hamlet joined in.

"But that wasn't a ghost!" Halley said.

"How do we know that?" Kyle said. "We have no idea what this 'Narrator' is."

"Either way, we don't have time for ghost hunts," Halley said. "We need to find the book so we can get home." She started searching the closest shelf.

Kyle looked at Hamlet. "What did you mean by saying you have to prove to your uncle that you're '*not* crazy or an irresponsible prankster'?" he asked.

Hamlet sighed. "Strange things keep happening around the castle—dogs meowing, bells tolling by themselves. Just a few days ago, this horrible stink came out of nowhere, and it's made the whole castle smell like five-week-old toad stew."

"Erch!" Gabe said in sympathy.

"It's clear that we're being haunted," Hamlet said. "But King Claudius keeps blaming these things on *me*, saying I'm just playing a bunch of pranks on the poor people of the castle."

He clenched his hands into fists. "When my father died, I should have become king. My uncle said I was too young, and that he would rule until I was old enough to take the throne, but as more time passes I think. . . ." He trailed off, frowning.

"Think what?" Halley prompted.

"I think he wants *my* job. Permanently," Hamlet explained. "If he can convince the kingdom that I will *never* be mature enough to rule and I will always seem insane, he might get away with it. I think he wants me to do something, *anything*, that he can use as an excuse to remove me from succession."

"To remove you from what?" Kyle said.

"To un-prince him," Halley explained. "What about your mom? Isn't she the queen?"

"Since she lost Dad, she's been a shadow of herself," Hamlet replied. "Barely talking, mostly keeping to her room. Claudius lets her stick around the court, probably to keep an eye on her. I'm sure she would like to help me, but she's not in any condition to. Besides, Claudius is very intimidating."

"And you *still* told him you think you saw a ghost?" Halley said. "That was silly."

Hamlet hung his head. "I *did* see a ghost. I thought if I explained that, it might prove to him that it wasn't *me* who put the minnows in the morning porridge, but it totally backfired.

Now the entire castle thinks I'm a liar, and
no one believes a word I say! They think *I'm*
responsible for the stink!"

He crossed his arms. "But I'm not. And I *did*
see a ghost. It's completely unfair that no one
believes me."

"Well, I'm sorry to hear that." Halley patted
him on the shoulder. "I can't imagine what that
must be like, having all the pressures of being
a prince. And *then* to have people think you're
not fit for it."

She looked at Kyle expectantly. It took Kyle a
moment to figure out what she was hinting at.

"*Oh!* Er, right . . . real bad. Very sad. Sorry
to hear it, dude. Prince! I mean, Prince." Kyle
punched Hamlet's shoulder. "Soooo . . . do you
think you could help us find our book? This is
the library, right?"

Halley glared at him. "Subtle."

She turned back to Hamlet. "What Kyle means to say is, could you please help us find a very important book we need?" She made what Kyle thought were supposed to be puppy eyes, but to him they looked more like guppy eyes.

Hamlet sighed glumly. "This room is just my private book collection. I spend most of my time here these days, so if a new book had appeared, I would've seen it. I could take you to the castle library, but remember how I said no travelers want to come here? Well, there's a reason. If my uncle finds out you came into the castle he might . . . well, you know."

93

"What?" Kyle asked.

"Let's put it this way," Hamlet said, straightening his cap. "He throws people in jail for frowning at him. He taxes people for walking on grass. He decrees that all birthday parties must be under twenty minutes long. Yesterday he had his chef plunged in pea soup until he almost drowned because there was too much salt on the potatoes. Imagine what would happen if we were *actually* caught doing something illegal?"

"Reega!" Gross Gabe said, even more garbly than usual.

"I think that's enough skulls," Kyle said, bending down. He grabbed a third of a sugar jaw out of his brother's hand.

"Raa!" Gabe said in frustration. "Wan snacksta-peez!"

Kyle frowned. That last word had sounded

suspiciously like *snacksterpiece*. Had his brother discovered his secret dessert stash? Mom always said that Gabe looked up to him . . . Kyle wondered if he'd accidentally taught his little brother unintended lessons about sugar intake.

"We'll discuss nutrition later," he said apologetically to Gabe. "Right now, we don't need you any more hyper than . . . wait a minute." Something was sticking out of Gross Gabe's mouth, and it wasn't a sweet skull. It was a wadded-up piece of paper.

Kyle gritted his teeth, reaching for it. He grabbed the paper with the tiniest parts of his fingers possible. It felt like picking something out of a lion's teeth. A really extra-slobbery lion. The ink was running, but he could just make out the words *prince of skulls*.

"It's the poem from the book!" Kyle yelled.

"You know what that m-means . . . ," Halley spluttered.

"YES," Kyle said.

Then he thought about it. "Wait, no. What does it mean? That my brother finally found something he can't destroy with his mouth? That the Narrator cast an anti-baby spell on the poem?"

"*No*," Halley said. "It means there might be a clue in the poem to tell us how to get home!" She quickly held it over the candle until it dried enough for her to open it and read again:

Listen! A prince of skulls cries in the dark—
Beware, for none see the ghostly mark.
To read or not to read, that is the question,
But first off, you must end the
prince's oppression.

Then flip the final page and reach "The End"
And soon enough, you will be home again.

"I'm pretty sure the bit in the first line, 'prince of skulls,' is about him," Halley said, pointing to Hamlet. "The next line is about a ghostly mark . . . which must be about Hamlet's ghost. Or whatever it really is."

"Like, the ghost is named Mark?" Kyle said.

"I don't think so," Halley said, and Kyle could see her fighting not to roll her eyes. "Probably it means 'mark' like writing, like a message or signature. Though with all the weird stuff going on, who knows?"

Kyle squinted. "It also says 'you must end the prince's oppression.' I don't think we can just find the book and leave. We have to help Hamlet *before* we read the end."

Halley sighed. "I can't believe I'm saying this, but you're probably right."

"So," Hamlet said slowly and carefully, "you'll help me?"

"Yes," Halley groaned. "I guess we have no choice. What's first?"

"First," Hamlet said, "you should put on dry clothes before you two get pneumonia."

"Noomona!" Gross Gabe said, reaching for another skull. Kyle grabbed it off the floor and Gabe glowered at him.

"I've got some spare stuff in here," Hamlet said. "Follow me."

He led them past a few shelves to a small back room, where he opened up a big trunk and started tossing out a variety of shirts, vests, and tights. Kyle held up the tights and stared at them. "These are for Halley, I guess."

"Nope," Hamlet said. "Those are for you! Girls wear long dresses. Only peasants and workers wear pants. If you want to blend in around the castle, you need these."

Halley laughed as Kyle shimmied into the tights. He knew now why they were called *tights*. They were tighter than a Gross Gabe welcome-home hug. He didn't understand why superheroes wore them. He could hardly *breathe*, much less stop a gang of reptilian men from robbing a bank.

When he was done adding a puffy shirt and vest, he wrapped his brother in a dry cloak.

"So," said Halley, an ice-cream-cone-shaped hat stuck on her head, "where do you, er, *find* a ghost?"

"Where there are dead people, I guess," Kyle said. "Hamlet, is there a graveyard nearby?"

"Yes, and that was the first place I saw the ghost," Hamlet said. "Come on." He picked up a big shovel. "We can't get caught," he said, hefting the shovel. "I'm going to pretend I'm a grave digger. Halley's hat should help her go unnoticed. And as for you . . ." Hamlet held out a spear.

Kyle's heart leaped with excitement. "Oh man!" he said. "Let me test out the spear!"

"Hold on," said Hamlet. "This thing's sharp, you know, and made for somebody a lot bigger.

Here"—he handed a metal knight's helmet to Kyle—"you look like a guard now."

"YES!" Kyle said, dropping the helmet onto his head. "I AM INVINCIBLE!" He triumphantly hoisted the spear into the air. It was much heavier than expected, and he immediately dropped it . . .

. . . onto his own head.

The echo of the spear smacking against the helmet rang in his ears and threw him off balance. He crashed to the floor, which only made it ring louder. Hmm, he'd have to take noise into account next time he drew a helmet for Mal or Cal.

Hamlet helped him to his feet, and Kyle took the spear in a shaking hand.

The helmet was made for a big man, and Kyle wasn't even particularly big for a boy. It came down too far over his eyes and ears. He could barely see or hear.

As they walked, Hamlet did his best to guide him by looking back over his shoulder at Kyle and giving directions.

"Left," Hamlet said. "Wait—go right! *Right!*"

Kyle clattered into a wall to his left, stumbled, and went right.

"Thanks a lot," he grumbled.

"Sorry," Hamlet said. "Duck."

"Where?" Kyle said. The helmet smacked into something and rang like a bell. "Oh, *duck.*" He ducked under the wall and kept going, more slowly this time.

"Door," he barely heard Hamlet say a minute later. He stopped as Hamlet reached past him to open a door.

At last, Kyle saw grass beneath his feet.

He felt like he was finally getting the hang of walking with the helmet on—when . . . *thud*!

"Uh-oh," Halley said.

Kyle pulled the helmet off his head to see what he'd hit.

And saw a wagon full of manure and chicken bones rolling down the hill away from them . . .

Oops.

Kyle followed the wagon's path with his eyes. With horror, he saw that it was going to collide with a tall, broad man standing at the bottom with a number of guards.

"Oh no," Hamlet said. "Oh no oh no oh no oh no!" He held the blade of the shovel up in front of his face to hide.

The tall man heard the cart just in time to turn around and watch it hit a rock, flip on its side, and dump its entire contents onto him and his guards.

Dun dun baaa!

"Really?" Halley said into the air. "That's the worst narrating I've ever heard."

Sorry, it's all I got.

"I hope that wasn't someone important," Kyle said nervously, through gritted teeth.

"Oh, um . . . ," Hamlet said. "Just my uncle Claudius. The king."

Kyle had just covered the king in manure.

CHAPTER EIGHT
OF ACCORDIONS AND KINGS

The king's long, slow march up the hill seemed to last forever. Every step shot a puff of dust into the air like a tiny meteor impact. They could hear his teeth grinding from twenty feet away. Every move shook little clumps of horse manure off him, rolling down his royal cloak and pattering around his feet.

Hamlet's knees shook. He pulled his hat as far down over his head as he could. Then he

scooped up some dirt from the ground and
rubbed it on his face until he looked like a
grave digger who'd broken his shovel and had
to finish with his teeth.

"Mmm urt!" Gross Gabe said, copying the
prince and smashing a clump of grass into his
forehead.

King Claudius pulled a wishbone out of
his hair, looked down at it, and crushed it to a
hundred tiny bits in his hand. He was a huge
man—his dark red robes could've made a tent,
and his nose looked like it could plow a
ten-acre field.

Thanks to Kyle's fumbling, the king *smelled*
like a ten-acre field. One growing a fresh crop
of outhouses.

"I once had a man's head for sneezing
on my green-bean casserole," he said in a

half hiss through his teeth. His hands were curled into tight, twitchy fists. "Who are you, and why should I not use your skulls for flowerpots in my delightful balcony garden?"

Kyle wished he could put his helmet back on and disappear into it. Instead his shaking hand let it thud to the ground.

"We're, um, from far away," Kyle said. "Uh, wagons are different where we come from. They're . . . more stable."

"And why were you *touching* one of my wagons to begin with?" Claudius asked, one eyebrow arching like a dark, fuzzy caterpillar. "Do you know the penalty for unlawful wagon-touching in *this* kingdom?" He finally let loose and screamed, "DO YOU?"

"Well," Kyle said, "well, um, we don't, but the wagon was—was . . ."

"S-s-s-scenery!" Halley chimed in, her teeth chattering worse than they had been in the freezing moat. "We're t-t-traveling performers, you see. W-we were r-rehearsing."

"Hursin!" Gross Gabe yelled.

"Yes, right," Kyle said. "We came, er . . . here to perform a play for . . . for you! Your Highness . . . ness."

"Hmph," Claudius said, fishing a drumstick bone from his robes. He dropped it to his feet and squashed it into the ground with his heel. "Plays are boring. My parents used to drag my brother and me to them. *He* loved them, the stuck-up little bookworm. All that fancy language and those silly gestures."

109

King Claudius was a very
harsh theater critic. The
last theater company that
came through got buried up to
their necks in sand next to
a colony of fire ants before
being banished from Denmark.
The only thing Claudius
cared about was Claudius.

"Yes, that's it!" Halley said. "This play is all about you! You and all of the amazing stuff you've done!"

"Yeah," Kyle said. "The true story of the great King Claudius! Our troupe travels to many countries around the globe, and people far and wide will know of your greatness!"

"Reeeeeally?" Claudius said, revealing rows

of chipped, crooked teeth. "That may be a little different, then. I've accomplished so much in my short reign. Making it illegal to brew tea on Tuesday. Making it mandatory for boiled stale radish to be included in every dinner. Taxing the use of the name Gary."

"Of course we'll be sure to include all of those," Halley said.

"Excellent," Claudius said. Kyle's trembling began to subside. Claudius cocked his head. "But why is this young grave-digging apprentice with you? Surely he is no actor."

Hamlet stayed still, not daring to budge from behind Halley, the shovel, or his hat.

"We're doing as much research as we can on your kingliness," Halley said, on a roll. "Including seeing the tombstones of everyone you've executed for their various terrible crimes." Kyle really didn't want to admit it, but Halley was in great form. He had to give her that, at least—she was helping save them from a horrible death.

"Ah, I hadn't thought of that!" Claudius said. "What a lovely idea. Be sure to look at Martin Anderssen's. I had his melon lopped off for daring to insult the accordion in my presence. I wanted to spit him on a pike, but my advisers suggested I reserve that for more serious crimes. As if there were such a thing! Next time I'll stick the offender myself. Just like this!"

Claudius yanked the spear from Kyle's hand and began to demonstrate, hopping around and stabbing the air.

Kyle's stomach tied up into knots. The king may have been more nuts than a family of squirrels in a pecan tree, but he could fight.

"Shineeey shineeeeey!"

Kyle had been so focused on the spear that he didn't see Gross Gabe crawl toward King Claudius until he was right under the spear tip.

"Look out!" Kyle cried.

His yell startled the king, who did a funny

half leap to avoid tripping over the tiny warrior. Claudius tumbled to the ground . . . and so did his crown.

And his hair.

Kyle, Halley, and Hamlet were as still as stone, staring bug-eyed at the king's naked head. He would have looked fine bald, except his head was covered in weird bumps and grooves. It looked like the surface of the moon.

Claudius's expression was totally blank, but Kyle imagined lava rumbling and boiling behind his eyes. The king's eyes went from Kyle to Halley to Gross Gabe—sizing each of them up for the chopping block. Even the royal guards were speechless and stood frozen with fear.

"Ba!"

Kyle jumped at the sound that erupted from King Claudius's mouth.

"Ba-ha ba-ha BA!"

At first Kyle thought Claudius was trying to impersonate a sheep, but then he realized the king was *laughing*.

"This child is a born jester!" he got out between *ba*s. "Brilliant! BA! You must have him perform, BA! Before your play! BA-HA BA-HA!"

"He's not really part of our act—" Halley's voice closed into a tiny squeak as the king's eyes narrowed to slits.

"I'm afraid that he must be in the play," Claudius said coolly, no longer baaing. "Actually, I'm not afraid. He *will* be part of the act—or *else*." He clasped his hands behind his back. "Do I need to remind you what *else* means in my kingdom?"

Kyle and Halley shook their heads very quickly.

115

"Good." Taking his crown—and wig—back, he shoved them onto his head and swept away, guards in tow.

"I think I just saw my life flash before my eyes," Kyle said. "It was . . . really boring."

"Be thankful you'll get to add more to it," Hamlet said, finally emerging from behind Halley and lowering his shovel. "That was very nearly the end."

"What a loathsome man!" Halley said.

Halley said the weirdest things sometimes. "I don't think he's made of bread," Kyle said.

"Not *loaf*-some, loathsome," Halley clarified. "Totally unlikable!"

Kyle scooped his brother up. His face was still covered in dirt and grass stains, and he was chewing on an acorn.

"I'm not sure if I should yell at you or thank you," Kyle said.

"Yellank!" Gabe said.

"Sounds about right."

"Okay, let's get to the graveyard and find the ghost," Halley said, "before anything else goes wrong."

```
Remember what the king
said. There's a lot of
"else" around here.
```

"Yeah, thanks," Kyle said, shaking his head.

```
Always glad to help a
character in need.
```

CHAPTER NINE
WALK LIKE A GHOST!

The oldest tombstones were so worn down, you couldn't read the names on them. They looked like crumbling teeth, sticking weakly out of the dirt. In the very middle of the graveyard were several huge stone crypts, with statues standing guard above them.

"Who's in there?" Kyle asked, pointing at the crypts.

"The biggest one's for the royal family," Hamlet said quietly. "My dad's buried there. And his parents, and their parents, for hundreds of years. The other ones are for dukes and barons and people like that."

He sniffed the air. "You smell that?"

"Yeah," Kyle said, crinkling his nose. "It's the same as the castle. Not as strong, though."

"So the ghost *is* causing the smell," Hamlet said confidently. He paused. "I think."

"How do you find a ghost?" Kyle asked.

"Maybe we have to call to it." Hamlet cleared his throat. "Um . . . Ghost? Are you here? Would you like to have a chat?"

"I think there's more to it than that," Halley said. "We need a ritual of some kind. Do you know any magical incantations?"

"Boodle doodle dee!" said Gross Gabe, wriggling in Kyle's arms.

"His guess is as good as mine," Hamlet said.

"Well, we have to do something," Kyle said. "This place gives me the creeps."

"There's one other thing I can think of . . . ," Halley said. "What if we pretend to be ghosts? Make it feel more comfortable, so it comes out to talk."

"I thought being a ghost was all about haunting live people," Kyle said.

"I still don't think ghosts exist," Halley said. "But if I were a ghost, I'd get tired of haunting people and would want to spend time with other ghosts."

"Absolutely," Hamlet said. "This graveyard has been here for centuries. There are many great Danes buried here. That is, Danish people, not dogs. They must have so much knowledge and history to share with each other."

"Okay." Kyle sighed and set his brother on the grass. "How do we start?"

"Can you make spooky noises, Gabey Wabey?" Halley said, bending down to be at eye level with him. "Wooooooo," she said, waggling her fingers. "Wooooo. You try it now."

Gabe studied her and then copied her finger waving, although it looked more like he was playing an invisible piano than pretending to be scary.

"Woooooooo!" he shrieked delightedly.

Halley dropped into a crouch, raised her arms over her head, and held them loosely so they looked like they were floating. She took slow, quiet steps.

"Woooo," she moaned. "I am doooomed to walk the eaaaaarth."

Kyle sighed again, thankful that the only witnesses were dead people. He followed Halley, trying to act like he was swimming through the air.

"Ooo," he said. "I, um, used to be alive, but now I'm noooot. . . ."

Hamlet got up onto a larger tombstone, swaying back and forth like he was hovering over it.

"See where I lie burieeeed," he said. "I wish they'd used a higher-quality topsoooooiiil. . . ."

"I feel really dumb," Kyle said.

"Woooooo!" Gross Gabe laughed.

"Shhh!" Halley said. "Focus on being spooky!"

Kyle focused on not tripping himself.

"Wooooookay, this is stupid," he said, slightly out of breath, although Gabe seemed to be just fine. Kyle didn't know if he'd inhaled even once.

"There's no gho—" Kyle stopped talking. A *creak* had come from beyond the tall grass.

A huge shadow moved toward them from behind one of the crypts. Long, wailing *creak*s and groans got louder and louder as the shadow grew.

They froze. A dark figure appeared, passing through the high grass between smaller stones. It looked like a man, but he wasn't walking.

He was *gliding*. And his clothes were ragged, covered in dirt, and torn—almost like he'd just clawed his way out of a grave.

CHAPTER TEN
PEE-EW!

The ghost opened its mouth, and Kyle winced, waiting for its bone-chilling howl.

"Hey, is this really the time and place for a sing-along?"

Kyle blinked. The ghost didn't sound ghosty—not that he really knew what a ghost would sound like. In fact, the ghost sounded like a normal man.

A few seconds later the figure emerged from

the tall grass, and Kyle saw why he sounded like a normal man: because he was one.

One very tall grave digger was standing in a wheelbarrow. Kyle could see a second, short and fat grave digger pushing it forward now that the tall grass and tombstones no longer hid them.

Kyle wasn't sure whether he was relieved or disappointed.

"Woooo-oomp!" Gross Gabe said as Kyle put a hand over his mouth.

"No more spooky now," Kyle said quietly before taking his hand away.

"No woo!" Gabe said, which seemed to make him just as happy.

"And you there, apprentice!" the fat one shouted as the wheelbarrow came to a squeaky halt. "Shouldn't you be over here helping us dig?"

"Er, yes," Hamlet said. "I was just showing them around."

"We're looking at different spots for graves!" Halley chimed in. "We're seeing what plots we might like. You know, the views, the neighbors, the decor. Your apprentice has been very helpful."

"Huh," the man in the wheelbarrow said.

"Some people really plan ahead, I guess. Though I admit it's necessary these days, with the graves being filled up so fast. I have to stand up in this wheelbarrow just to spot new spaces to dig! So what was all that dancing and singing?"

"Stretching and breathing exercises!" Kyle said. "This damp air gets into the joints, you know? We had to stop for a minute to limber up."

The grave digger nodded, though his puzzled look didn't go away. Somewhere off in the trees a crow cawed.

"By the way," Hamlet said casually, "you gentlemen don't happen to have seen any ghosts recently, have you? Maybe in the past few days?"

Both grave diggers started to laugh.

"Everyone always asks us about ghosts," said the barrow pusher. "My boy, if there are ghosts, they've sure never felt like talking to us. Even if they *were* real, I imagine they'd have better things to do than hang around where they got buried."

"The only funny business we've seen is somebody sneaking around in a hooded cloak with bags of redcap mushrooms and bundles of skunkblossom," the other one added. "Don't know why. Everyone knows redcaps are poisonous and the only thing a skunkblossom does is smell like eight weeks of sheep farts in a wine cask."

The grave digger shrugged. "But with the way the castle smells now, who'd even notice, anyway?"

"True," said the other. "All because of Prince Hamlet! Did you hear he's blaming a ghost for the stench?"

"That's nuts!" The tall one snorted. "Good thing ol' Claudius took over. He may not be a nice king, but at least he knows which way is up without a map. You all right there, apprentice?"

Kyle glanced at Hamlet. The prince was shaking so hard, his shovel was kicking up dirt puffs.

"He's just chilly," Kyle said, stepping in front of him. "Like we said, dampness and everything."

"Well, we'd better be off," said the barrow pusher. "Have a good, uh, tour. Let us know if you have any questions."

The grave diggers creaked away with the wheelbarrow.

"It wasn't a ghost, but it was a clue," Halley said. "I bet skunkblossom was what made the castle smell bad in the first place. Where does it grow around here?"

Kyle looked expectantly at Hamlet, but the prince didn't say anything. He was too busy fuming.

"I can't believe how unfair this all is," Hamlet said, glowering. "It's not right that I'm accused without being proven guilty. I can't believe this is legal!"

"It's probably not," Halley interrupted smoothly, "which is why we must get you undeniable proof that you're innocent and fit to be king. Which way to the skunkblossoms?"

"Follow me," Hamlet said. Though he was still glowering, he began to walk. They crunched through the tall grass toward an area near the opposite side of the wall. "The first time I saw the ghost, it appeared in the middle of the graveyard and drifted in this direction, right toward . . . this spot." He sniffed the air. "And this smell!"

"Yeah," Kyle said, wrinkling his nose, "I noticed." It was the same smell that made the castle seem like a walk through a swamp inhabited by nervous skunks.

Growing against the wall was a large patch of dark-green, yellow-splotched plants with bright bulblike flowers. They were almost pretty—if you could stand getting close enough to look.

"Fowers!" Gross Gabe said, trying to shake free of Kyle.

"No, no, no," Kyle said, tightening his grip. "Smelling bad is basically your job. You really don't need any help."

They walked up to the patch, glancing left and right for any sign of a hooded figure.

"Look!" Hamlet said. "There's a big empty spot right over here."

The empty patch was large—and Kyle thought that a lot of skunkblossoms could have fit in there. Maybe even enough to stink up the whole castle.

```
They pondered the possibility
that a distilled skunkblossom
reduction left to simmer
until properly coagulated
might just do the trick.
```

"What?" Kyle said. "What did any of that mean?"

```
It meant yes. If, say, a
hooded figure had that many
skunkblossoms, he could boil
them into a really awful
potion that would stink
up the entire castle.
```

"Hey," Halley said, "there's something here." Holding her breath, she crouched down and brushed aside some fallen leaves.

Underneath was a very clear footprint.

"What kind of ghost leaves a footprint?" Hamlet asked, baffled.

"No kind," Halley said. "Hamlet, you're not seeing a ghost—you've been tricked!"

CHAPTER ELEVEN
ROSES ARE RED, VIOLETS ARE BLUE, SKUNKBLOSSOMS SMELL—JUST LIKE YOU!

"I feel so stupid!" Hamlet said, looking down in dismay. Kyle felt pretty dumb, too. How many times had he drawn Mal and Cal Worthy looking at the ground for mysterious footprints like they had in issue five? Why hadn't he thought of looking down sooner?

"No, it's okay," Halley said. "If it's not a ghost, then it's a person—and people can't walk

"SOMETHING HAD BEEN THROUGH THE DARK VALLEY. SOMETHING BIG AND ANGRY—PROBABLY BECAUSE IT COULD NEVER FIND SHOES IN ITS SIZE." —*THE ASTOUNDING ADVENTURES OF MAL & CAL WORTHY*, ISSUE #5. WORDS BY BECCA DEED, ILLUSTRATIONS BY KYLE WORD.

through walls or disappear. We can catch the actual prankster and prove you're not lying!"

"And then we'll be able to go home," Kyle added. "The grave digger said this person's been here a couple of times, and last time he chased him away. That means he may well come back again soon."

"Fowers!" Gross Gabe proclaimed, struggling to get out of Kyle's grasp.

"We can set a trap," Halley said. She pointed to Hamlet's grave-digging shovel. "And we have just the tool to do it with."

"You really think that will work?" Hamlet said.

"Don't know," Halley said, "but it worked in *Deadly Whispers* issue number forty-three."

"True," Kyle said. "It . . ." He stopped cold.

Had Halley just referenced a comic book? Could it be that she had a non-obnoxious interest? He was about to ask, but she was already halfway across the skunkblossom patch, looking for a good spot with Hamlet. There was no time to ask about it now, but he made a mental note in very bold mental pen to ask later.

Setting the trap was a several-step process. First they had to dig up one large skunkblossom plant without damaging it and set it carefully to the side. Then the work truly began.

Hamlet, Kyle, and Halley took turns with the shovel, and whoever didn't have it did as best they could with their hands. In Gross Gabe's case, that was actually pretty good. He flung soil from the growing pit like flinging dirt was his favorite game. Which it was.

Kyle wished he could harness the energy his brother had playing with dirt. With the right machinery, it could probably open a portal back to the real world.

"Now comes the tricky part," Halley said when they were done.

They covered the opening of the pit with a thin layer of sticks and leaves and spread just a few inches of dirt on top of that. Then they stuck the skunkblossom in the very center.

"Not superconvincing," Halley said. "But in the dark, it should do the trick."

"All right," Hamlet said. "Let's hide and wait." They hurried behind the nearest tombstone big enough to conceal them.

Time passed. It got very dark. Kyle's stomach started to growl, and he tried covering it with his hands to muffle the noise. The only other noises were from the occasional owl and tiny scurrying things Kyle didn't want to think about. Hamlet tapped his feet and drummed his fingers on the tombstone.

"Think they're coming tonight?" Kyle asked.

"Seems unlikely now," said Halley. "It took us a long time to dig. Anyone could've spotted us and run away."

"I don't know," Hamlet said. "Should we stay or should we go?"

"I say we stay put," Kyle said. "We worked hard on that trap. We should at least give it till morning."

"Hey," Hamlet said, "hold on. . . ."

Halley ignored him. "Who knows what this mysterious person will do during that time?" she said, her whisper getting less whisper-like.

"But this is the only place we know to look," Kyle said. "Besides, the trap was *your* idea!"

"Wait, both of you," Hamlet said anxiously.

"My idea to help us get out of a situation that *you* got us into," Halley said. "The kid can barely spell his own name, but *he* gets a magical book delivered to his front door!"

ALAS, POOR HIM

"*SHH!*" Hamlet ordered. They shushed. And in the silence, they heard the sound of sticks breaking, a *thump*, and a surprised yelp.

Hamlet smiled. "We got him!"

CHAPTER TWELVE
A RUSTLE IN THE BUSHES IS NEVER A GOOD SIGN. . . .

The trap had worked perfectly.

Carefully, Kyle crept toward the pit, clutching Gross Gabe closely to him. Hamlet and Halley followed right behind, almost crawling. After all, whoever was in there was obviously up to no good. Maybe it was an evil knight who would leap right out of the pit, two swords flashing through the air. That'd make a good villain, actually. He'd have to tell Becca about it.

He peeked over the edge very slowly. At the bottom of the pit was a small, cloaked figure—a figure much smaller than he'd expected.

The figure looked up and pulled back the hood to reveal the angry face of a girl.

Kyle was surprised. She looked about their age, and not evil at all. Just really grumpy about falling into a pit trap.

"Ophelia!" Hamlet exclaimed.

"Hamlet?" The girl—Ophelia—got to her feet and looked suspiciously up at Halley, Kyle, and Gross Gabe. "What are you doing here?"

"I think *you're* the one who needs to answer that question." Hamlet crossed his arms. "Why are you sneaking around the skunkblossom patch? Are you the one setting off stink bombs in the castle?"

"No way," Ophelia said. "I came here to try and find out who did!"

Hamlet tilted his head. "Three days ago the castle started to smell, and I haven't seen you in three days. So even though you're my best friend, I have to ask . . . where *were* you?"

Ophelia brushed dirt from her cloak. "Unlike *some* mopey princes in this castle," she huffed, glaring at Hamlet, "I actually work. I'm teaching poetry by mail to an Italian kid. I've been writing notes and examples to send back to him."

"For three days?" Kyle asked.

"He . . . needs a lot of notes," Ophelia said. "He's getting better, slowly. Very slowly. I have the letters to prove it!"

Hamlet looked unsure, but Halley nodded. "We believe you," she said. "Give us a second and we'll help you out of there."

A soft *snap* made Kyle turn his head. Was someone else in the skunkblossom patch with them? He listened again, but all he heard was Gross Gabe's soft snoring in his arms. It seemed the digging had worn him out.

Hamlet and Halley lowered the shovel into the pit, and Ophelia grabbed hold. With their help, she climbed out. Ophelia looked curiously at Kyle and Halley.

147

"Who are these people, anyway?"

"I'm Kyle," Kyle said with a small wave. "This is a snoring machine my parents tell me is my brother," he went on, gesturing to Gross Gabe.

"Deeble dee," Gross Gabe mumbled sleepily.

"I'm Halley," Halley said. "We're not from here."

"Well, wherever you're from, I suggest you go back," Ophelia said. "Elsinore's not a great place to be right now, thanks to that awful King Claudius."

She shook more dirt from her long dress. "He's eliminated or imprisoned a lot of people, and he's made so many awful new laws! He decreed that tennis be called *green orb smack tag* now. Using the word *tennis* is punishable by up to five years in prison.

"If a dog runs away, its owner is forced to adopt fifteen cats. And writers are forced to buy ink from his own royal shop, where it's more expensive than silver!"

She stomped her foot. "It's so unfair! I've barely been able to smuggle enough from outside Denmark to keep up with my poetry lessons, and there's none leftover for my own work! I wish that he would just—"

A bright, flickering light filled the skunkblossom patch, momentarily blinding Kyle.

But as his vision cleared, he almost wished it hadn't.

King Claudius stepped through the trees.

His guards were holding lanterns. The yellow-orange light made his crown sparkle and glint as he shook his head with mock sadness.

"Why oh why am I not surprised?" he said,

the lantern light giving his face jack-o'-lantern shadows. "I suspected Ophelia was up to no good, so I followed her, and look who I find."

Kyle looked at Hamlet and his heart sank. The prince had taken off the floppy hat to dig the pit, and his face was completely exposed.

"Your royal splendiferousness," Ophelia said, suddenly bobbing around like she was off balance and pitching her voice weirdly high. "I was just out picking some flowers!"

She grabbed a skunkblossom plant and held it up. "Look! Daisies!"

"My dear Ophelia," Claudius said. "Your little 'silly poet' act may fool some people around here, but not me. I also know you've been slinking off to meet one of the dastardly ink smugglers. Because I do not have proof, *yet*," he growled, "I'll go easy. Tomorrow, you will clean every tapestry in the castle. With the teeniest, tiniest brush I can find. And as for you, little Hammie . . ."

"My name is *Hamlet*," Hamlet whispered.

"I'm afraid I have far graver crimes to accuse you of," the king said, then paused and chuckled. "Ba-HA! *Grave*. Dear me, I'm clever. I'm a poet and, er, I'm not even aware of it."

He cleared his throat. "Anyway. I shall now read the crimes of which you stand accused." Reaching into his robes, King Claudius pulled out a scroll. It unrolled from his hand to the ground. "*First,* you are accused of creating general chaos and disruption, as well as trying to cause fear and panic by filling the castle with a foul stink potion."

"But I didn't—" Hamlet protested.

"*Second*," Claudius continued, "you are

accused of trying to blame all your actions on a ghost, causing even more fear and panic in the castle."

"But I didn't—"

"*GUILTY!*" King Claudius shouted. In Kyle's arms, Gross Gabe woke up. "Sorry, there's some more legal stuff I could have said, but I decided to save time and cut to the chase."

Kyle exchanged nervous glances with Halley as the king rolled up the accusations. Whatever the king said next, he knew it wouldn't be good.

"You know, Hammie," King Claudius said, "disrupting the royal government could be considered treason. The punishment for which is beheading. Lucky for you, I am horribly, *terribly* merciful." Claudius sighed dreamily at his own mercy. "So it's boarding school for you!"

Hamlet looked horrified and even Halley winced.

"You'll be locked in your quarters tonight," Claudius continued. "And you'll be on the first ship to England tomorrow. I hear the food there is"—his face twisted up like a raisin—"*delicious.*

Mushed peas and stale bread and dried fish. *Mmm.*"

One of the guards took hold of Hamlet in a big, armored fist.

"Shineey shineey!" Gross Gabe suddenly yelled. He pushed free of Kyle's loose grip and crawled toward Claudius, his eyes on the sparkling crown.

Kyle lunged to reel him in, but Claudius got

there first. In one swoop, he grabbed Kyle's brother.

"As for you, little jester," the king cooed, "it's time for *you* to start earning your keep. You'll come back with me."

"But, but—" Kyle protested.

"You two 'actors' can go," Claudius said. "Where is up to you. Maybe try Italy. I hear Verona is in need of performers this time of year. But if I ever see you again, I'm going to dunk you in strawberry jam and toss you in a pit of weasels."

"Do weasels even like strawberries?" Halley said.

Kyle winced. Now was *not* the time to be asking questions.

"*Silence!*" Claudius said. "My point is, I will

do whatever I like with you. Whether or not it makes sense. I bid you all good night!"

With that, he spun around and walked away with his guards, Hamlet, Kyle's baby brother, and any hope Kyle had of ever getting home.

CHAPTER THIRTEEN
THE SKULL AND CROSSBONES ISN'T A GOOD SIGN, EITHER

"How could you just let him take Gabe like that?!" Halley said.

"Instead of doing what?" Kyle said. "Fighting three armed guards? I'd be vulture breakfast on the castle walls tomorrow. I didn't see you jumping them, either!"

"True," she said. "But *you* got us into this mess in the first place."

"How many times do we have to argue about

that?" Kyle said, kicking a rock into the pit. It made a dull *thump-thump* as it fell to the bottom. "*I* didn't order that book. It just came. It's that Narrator person's fault we're here. What kind of guy is this, anyway? Who would spend their time tricking kids into horrible, awful-smelling castles full of skulls and evil kings?"

And snakes. Don't
forget the snakes.

"Gaahh!" Kyle shouted, grabbing a handful of leaves and hurling them into the air.

"And why *us*?" Halley said. "Other than my appreciation for Shakespeare and general intellect, of course."

Kyle wanted to say something about all the

good her *general intellect* had done, but he let it drop. He was too tired to keep fighting Halley when there was an evil king to deal with. He *had* to get his baby brother back. What would Cal Worthy do in this situation?

Something I can't do, he thought angrily. *That's why Becca and I created Mal and Cal Worthy in the first place. It's why I'm real and they're not.*

"I can't let him send Hamlet away," Ophelia said fervently.

Kyle jumped. He'd been so lost in his own thoughts, he'd almost forgotten she was there.

"He's the rightful king," Ophelia went on. "He's the only symbol of hope we have left."

158

"Then I guess we'd better go save him," Halley said.

Ophelia nodded, pulling her hood back up. Out of the moonlight, her face disappeared into shadow.

"I can help you," Ophelia said. "After all, I accidentally led Claudius here. This is all as much my fault as anyone's."

"What do we do?" Kyle said, rubbing his arms. It was starting to get cold.

"There are secret passages in the castle," Ophelia said. "We can get around without being seen."

"Okay," Halley said. "Lead on."

They walked back to the castle in silence and tiptoed across the lowered drawbridge. They snuck along the wall and entered through the side door Hamlet had taken them out through earlier.

Ophelia looked left and right down the dark corridor before pushing a stone in the opposite wall. A door swung open just enough for them to duck through.

"I haven't used these in a while," she said. "But Hamlet's chambers should be this way. . . ."

The secret passage went up, leveled out, and hit an intersection. Ophelia took them down the left fork.

"Why are these here, anyway?" Kyle whispered.

"If an invading force takes over the castle, we can hide and move around secretly to try and take it back," Ophelia explained, the hood still hiding her face.

They kept going in silence. The secret corridors were lit only by tiny bits of light that came through small gaps. Kyle kept bumping his head on stones that stuck unevenly down from the ceiling. Most grown-ups would've had to crawl.

"This should let us out right next to Hamlet's room," Ophelia said, and slowly pushed another door open.

"Huh," Ophelia said as she stepped out.

"Huh what?" Kyle asked, as they followed. The hall they were in wasn't much bigger than the secret passage and was only slightly better lit.

"I must have taken a wrong turn somewhere," she said. "I don't think I've ever seen this part of the castle before."

"Look over there," Kyle said, pointing to a lonely torch next to an iron door at the end of the little corridor. They walked to it. On the door was an unmistakable symbol: a skull and crossbones.

Kyle gulped. "I think that's the symbol for . . ."

Looking pale, Halley finished his sentence: ". . . poison."

CHAPTER FOURTEEN
OKAY, SOMETHING EVIL IS DEFINITELY HAPPENING IN DENMARK!

Ophelia opened the iron door carefully.

Inside, a dim lantern was nestled in the corner of a little room—a little room filled with shelves and shelves of flasks, vials, and jars. They had labels like *Moat Snakes' Venom*, *Redcap Mushroom Serum*, *Liquid Heart Attack*, and *Problem-Solving Powder (Just add to any beverage!)*.

"Wow," Kyle said. Or tried to say. His

mouth was hanging open, so it was more like "Oahhohhhh."

"There's enough poison to kill every person in Elsinore," Ophelia gasped. "It must belong to Claudius! What's he doing with all of this?"

"The question is, what's he *going* to do with it?" Kyle asked.

"And look over there!" Halley pointed to a table covered in skunkblossom and balls of mozzarella cheese that looked like they were older than the castle itself. Even from this distance, Kyle thought its awful stench made Gabe seem like a bundle of flowers wrapped in fresh laundry.

Gabe.

Just thinking of his little brother made Kyle's stomach hurt. He had completely failed as a big brother. Gabe might smell bad, but he was still family . . . and he'd actually been helpful. If it weren't for Gabe, they wouldn't have had the Narrator's poem or been able to dig the trap in the graveyard so quickly.

And what had Kyle done? He hadn't protected his brother, that was what!

Kyle needed to save Gabe from Claudius, and once he had, he'd make sure the little dude played safely.

"Now we know who's been making stink bombs," Ophelia said grimly. "It wasn't Hamlet or a ghost. It was Claudius!"

"You're right." Halley nodded. "I think he's been trying to frame Hamlet the whole time!"

"We've got to rescue Hamlet," Ophelia said, closing her eyes.

"And Gabe," Kyle reminded them.

They sped through the secret corridors,

twisting left and right, then left again, until they reached a small panel. Ophelia pushed the panel open, and they emerged into a large, well-lit hallway decorated with tapestries and velvet couches. Halfway down the hall, an armored guard stood outside a door. He looked very bored.

"There's no way we can sneak past him," Halley whispered.

"It's okay," Ophelia said. "There's a back entrance. This way."

They turned a corner into a hallway that was empty except for one tall cabinet. Ophelia braced her shoulder against it and shoved. It squeaked along the polished floor to reveal a small, dusty door behind it.

"It's just an empty cabinet painted to look fancy." Ophelia pulled a key ring from her belt. "When Claudius took over, I knew it wouldn't be long before he found a way to get rid of Hamlet. No one pays attention to quiet poets like me, so I've been able to prepare."

She unlocked the door and led them into a cramped, dark room. Kyle slid the cabinet back in place and closed the door.

"This is Hamlet's closet," Ophelia said.

"Why aren't there any clothes in it?" Kyle said.

"There are," Ophelia said. "They're just hard to see. He wears a lot of black. Now hold on and give me a moment to tell him—"

The doors swung open with a *bang*!

"Who's there? Stand still or I'll . . . I'll stick you!"

The torchlight blinded Kyle, but as he blinked his eyes, Hamlet's bedroom came into focus. And so did Hamlet.

And the trout the prince was holding like a club.

"It's us!" Halley shouted.

"Oh." Hamlet lowered the fish. "Are you hungry? I was just about to eat. Might be my last decent meal for a long time."

"We're here to help you," Halley said.

"I'm afraid there's no way to help," Hamlet said sadly as he waved them into his bedroom. "The world is an unfair place. My uncle stole my kingdom and that's all there is to it." He dropped the fish back onto its plate with a sad *splat*.

"Claudius took me in front of his council of advisers," he continued. "I tried to tell them that someone else set off the stink bombs, and not me, but Claudius said I was losing my mind. He said I need to leave for a while to regain my senses, and *everyone* agreed!"

His shoulders slumped. "That's how good he is at this. He's on the verge of robbing me of my rightful place, of my father's legacy, of everything I was supposed to be when I grew up. Now *I'm* even starting to doubt that I can handle the throne."

"You *can* do it," Kyle said. "We discovered a secret storeroom Claudius has been using. It's filled with poison *and* skunkblossom. *He's* the one who set off the stink bombs."

"Unfortunately," Ophelia said, lowering her hood at last, "I have no idea where it is. We found it by accident after several wrong turns in the secret passages. I don't know if I could find it again, even if I looked for days."

"I've only got until morning," Hamlet said somberly.

"At least we can sneak you out of here," she said.

"I don't want to run away," Hamlet said. "Claudius will just use that as more evidence against me, and then I'll never be able to come back. It's so unfair! That's my throne!"

"How can we prove to them that you're not seeing things?" Halley said. She smoothed a wrinkle on the tablecloth as she thought. "Psychology doesn't even exist yet!"

Kyle furrowed his forehead and felt two

lines appear between his eyebrows. Becca called them his thinking lines. He wished Becca were here now to help him come up with a plan. When they wrote *Mal & Cal* together, they'd ask each other questions about what they saw in front of them and use the answers to come up with new settings and characters.

With his heart already sinking, he looked around the room. Ophelia was tapping her chin, while Halley continued to smooth out wrinkles in the tablecloth.

"Wait a second," Kyle said. "Hamlet, pick up your plate and glass."

"Why?"

"Just do it!"

Hamlet shrugged and lifted his dinner and glass off the table. Kyle took the white tablecloth and held it up.

"There's another way they'll believe Hamlet's not crazy," he said with a grin. "If they see the ghost themselves!"

For the first time ever, Halley looked confused. "What? You want to show them the ghost of all dinners past?"

"No," Kyle said, waving the tablecloth a little. "I want to show them Hamlet's ghost. Nobody believes Hamlet, right? We need proof. If we don't have evidence on hand, we'll *make* some."

"We'll defeat Claudius's lie with our own lie," Ophelia said with a grin. "I like it."

Kyle nodded. "First we get the council on Hamlet's side. *Then* we can take them to Claudius's poison chamber."

Halley got a gleam in her eye. Usually when that happened, Kyle would brace himself for a thirty-minute lecture on German grammar or who knows what else, but now he was excited to hear her idea.

"We can be like the men in the graveyard," she said. "If we can get a wheelbarrow, two of us can stand in it, one on the other's shoulders, under the sheet. It'll look like a ghost is floating through the castle."

"I like the way you're thinking, Pierce-Blossom." Kyle nodded with approval. "Let me see. . . . Hamlet, do you have ink and paper?"

"Paper," Hamlet said, taking a sheet out from a small desk along with a feather quill, "but like Ophelia said, ink is hard to come by these days."

"I have some," Ophelia said, pulling a small ink pot from a cloak pocket and handing it to Kyle. "Don't spill any—it cost me my pearl bracelet!"

Kyle quickly sketched out what he was thinking.

"I'm impressed, Kyle," Halley said, looking over his shoulder. "I didn't realize you could draw! I like your style. Almost reminds me of Ben Templesmith."

Kyle's favorite comic book artist.

"Thanks," he said, mystified. "If . . . if we ever get home, we should talk about artists and comics sometime." He braced himself in case a time-traveling Kyle from the past appeared and tackled him for suggesting he voluntarily spend time with Halley.

"Yeah," she said, nodding, looking surprised herself. "That might be fun." She picked up Kyle's drawing and showed it to Hamlet and Ophelia. "So how do we make this happen?"

Everything came together quickly. Kyle and

Halley cut eyeholes in the tablecloth while
Ophelia snuck back out of the closet to get a
wheelbarrow.

When she reappeared through the closet
a few minutes later with a wheelbarrow just
big enough for someone to stand in, she also
passed out a small handful of something
sticky and green. "Crushed mint leaves," she
explained. "Stuff it in your nostrils so the castle
smell doesn't distract you."

They crept back out through the closet.
Ophelia helped Halley get onto Hamlet's
shoulders as Kyle held the wheelbarrow steady.
Halley unfurled the sheet and draped it over
herself and Hamlet, adjusting it until the
eyeholes lined up with her eyes.

Kyle's first step made him realize his insides
were sloshing around. He hadn't used the

bathroom since they'd gotten there. All that moat water and tea he'd had were catching up to him.

"Hold on, is there a bathroom nearby?" he asked.

"You want a bath?" Hamlet said. "With all this stink, it's not like anyone will notice if you need one, anyway."

"No, no," Kyle said. "I have to pee."

"Why didn't you say so?" Ophelia said. "There's a chamber pot right over there." She pointed back into Hamlet's closet.

"What's a . . . ," Kyle said, then saw what she was pointing at. A ceramic thing halfway between a flowerpot and a salad bowl. "That?! That's my option?"

He stared at the chamber pot and thought about it. He really had to go, but . . .

To pee, he thought. *Or not to pee. That is the question.*

"Hey!" Ophelia said, snapping her fingers in Kyle's face. "Time's up. We have to go."

```
And so, with a stomach full
of dread and an even fuller
bladder, Kyle began to push
the wheelbarrow to his doom.
```

"Hang on," Kyle whispered. "To my WHAT?"

```
Just go with it! Tension
makes the story better!
```

Kyle's bladder was now painfully full. There
was probably enough water in him to fill the
Shadow Sea, a place of jet-black currents and
sea monsters that Mal and Cal Worthy fought in
issue seven.

"Fine!" he gasped, hopping. "Just hurry up
the narration and get me to the restroom soon,
okay?"

```
What do you think I'm trying
to do? Ahem, where were we
. . . oh, right. Kyle pushed the
wheelbarrow toward his doom.
```

"THE WORTHIES DESCENDED HUNDREDS OF FEET INTO THE WATERY DEPTHS AND CAME FACE TO BUS-SIZE FACE WITH THE SERPENT QUEEN OF FATHOMOPOLIS." —*THE ASTOUNDING ADVENTURES OF MAL & CAL WORTHY*, ISSUE #7.

WORDS BY BECCA DEED, ILLUSTRATIONS BY KYLE WORD.

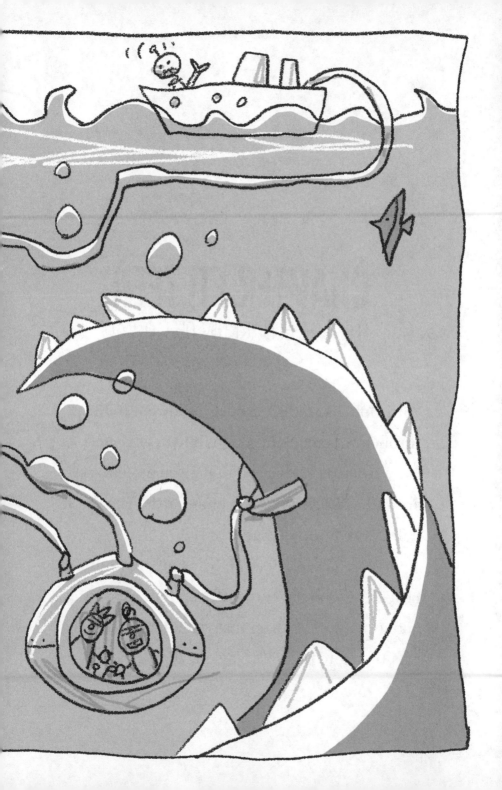

CHAPTER FIFTEEN
THE WHEELBARROW OF DOOM!

With Ophelia leading the way, they got to the throne room much faster than Kyle expected. Only twice did Kyle have to jog the wheelbarrow around a corner to hide from guards. The castle halls were mostly empty.

"Where is everybody?" Kyle said, breathing heavily. He had never really been into gardening, and it *really* didn't help that it felt like Lake Erie was trying to push its way out of him. That, and the adrenaline of terror, were keeping him wide-awake even though he should have been exhausted. It had been a really long day.

As he moved the wheelbarrow, he focused on the task at hand, trying hard not to think about running faucets, waterfalls, roof gutters in a rainstorm, out-of-control fire hoses. . . .

"Thanks for making this easier," Kyle muttered, sweat beads forming on his forehead.

This is nothing. You should see what Becca, Sam, and Rufus are facing in Romeo and Juliet's Verona.

"What?" Kyle gasped. "Becca is trapped in a bookworld, too?!"

"Claudius is holding court," Hamlet whispered from under the tablecloth. Kyle turned his attention back to him. He'd figure out what the Narrator meant later.

"Everyone important enough to be there is in his throne room," Hamlet explained. "I mean, *my* throne room."

It was only the second or third time Kyle had heard Hamlet say that he was the real king. He didn't strike Kyle as somebody who really wanted to rule. . . . Then again, just because you don't *think* you like something doesn't mean you wouldn't be mad if someone *stole* that something away from you. Kyle understood that only too well.

Gabe was loud, smelly, and annoying—but

there were good parts, too. The funny noises
he made were actually very inventive, and
he had this nice habit of always laughing at
Kyle's jokes. It would be great to get Hamlet his
throne, but they *had* to save Gabe.

"Stop here," Ophelia whispered. In front of
them was a long balcony overlooking what was
clearly the throne room, based on the sounds
and the number of voices drifting up.

"The railing is high enough to hide the
wheelbarrow," Kyle said, nodding. "People will
look up and they'll just see our ghost."

"And it's far enough away that it won't be
obvious it's two kids under a cloth," Ophelia
said. "Especially with the smoke from the
torches drifting up here."

"You two ready?" Kyle said, tapping Halley
on the back.

"All set," she said. Her voice was muffled beneath the tablecloth.

"Ready when you are," Hamlet said.

Kyle looked back at Ophelia, who nodded. He hefted the handles and pushed.

As he tried to control the wobble of the wheelbarrow, Kyle caught glimpses of the party below through gaps in the railing. Even this late into the evening, lords and ladies frolicked around huge banquet tables in bright-colored clothes. Red-and-white striped dresses, yellow coats with green buttons, hats with ostrich feathers. Some of the men even had striped or polka-dotted tights.

The fancy clothes looked pretty silly by themselves, but adding to the silliness were the handkerchiefs. Everybody had one tied over his or her nose and mouth.

Thanks to the mint in his nose, Kyle couldn't tell what the general smell level of the castle was.

It clearly was still pretty bad.

A small band played in one corner, and Claudius stood near the band, clapping not quite in time to the rhythm. The band kept changing tempo to match his claps, because he was the king—and a terrifying one at that.

Claudius was the only one without a handkerchief tied to his face. He seemed to just be gritting his teeth and pretending there was no smell.

"Nobrolee! Nobrolee!"

Gabe's voice pierced the crowd's noise, and Kyle finally spotted the toddler. He was sitting on one of the tables in a full jester outfit, shaking broccoli stalks like maracas.

Rage flooded Kyle's veins.

Gabe hated broccoli! Kyle was pretty sure he'd heard him having nightmares about it. His jaw clenched. Nobody tortured his brother with broccoli! (Other than him. Two or three times. But that was different.)

Kyle kept going, wondering if anyone had seen them yet. And as though the crowd had heard his question, he finally heard gasps.

"What is that?" a woman shrieked from below.

```
Looks like you've been spotted!
Oh, this is so exciting!
```

Kyle wanted to say something, but he needed his breath to push the wheelbarrow. He settled for rolling his eyes.

"It's just . . . drifting!" a man said.

"It can't be," King Claudius gasped. The band stopped. He stared up at them, going almost as pale as the sheet over Hamlet and Halley. "It can't be . . . *Hamlet?*"

Kyle panicked. "He knows it's you!"

"No," Hamlet whispered from under the sheet. "Hamlet was my dad's name, too."

"We better scram before he sends the guards up here," Halley whispered.

"Just a little farther," Ophelia said. "Then we'll hit the end of the balcony and 'disappear.'"

Kyle was sweating with effort. They were so close!

But the pressure on his bladder was enormous. He began to do a little tap dance, hopping from one foot to the other. . . .

"Watch out!" Halley yelled.

But it was too late.

The wheelbarrow fell to the left, hitting a weak point in the railing. The old stone crumbled, and Hamlet, Halley, and the wheelbarrow plunged through it, pulling Kyle and Ophelia along with them. They fell in a

huge heap onto a banquet table.

SKKKRONCHH!

The room spun as Kyle

got to his feet, pulling the sheet from around his head. He was covered in goose grease, raisins, bits of parsley, and various other food scraps.

And King Claudius was glowering at them.

And the guards all pointed their sharp spears at them.

And Kyle *still* had to pee.

CHAPTER SIXTEEN
THE RETURN OF PRINCE HAMMIE

"I knew it!" King Claudius yelled as the kids scrambled to their feet. "I knew it!"

Despite the fact that he was covered in a not-so-regal crown of parsley, Hamlet drew himself up to his full four feet and one and a half inches.

"I'm not going to England!" Hamlet announced. "I'm the rightful king! You all know that. When my father died, the crown should've come to me."

"When my *dear* brother died, Hammie," Claudius said, "you were too young to rule. It was my job to run things until you were fit to take over."

He looked around at the whole court. Then he raised both hands toward Hamlet. "You've raved about a ghost floating around. And even more alarming, you've set off stink bombs so pungent that people can barely walk through the castle without passing out!"

The king jabbed his finger at Hamlet. "The royal court and myself are unable to properly rule because we must choke our way through every function and meeting. Denmark is on the verge of collapse, and now, to top everything off, you've put on this *puppet* show!"

"That's a lie!" Kyle said, as he scanned the

banquet hall looking for his brother. "*You* set off the stink bombs. We can prove it, too."

"Oh?" Claudius sneered. "Let's see your proof."

"We don't have it with us," Halley said, "but we've seen it. If you'll just listen . . ."

"Ba-HA! Ba-HA ha-HA!" Claudius laughed, but not very nicely. "Do you think we have the memory of a goldfish? *You* were just caught red-handed *faking* evidence."

As Claudius spoke, more and more of his guards appeared in the room. Kyle looked frantically, but he didn't see his brother anymore. The only people he could see were the lords and ladies, who had made a wide circle around them, wearing expressions that told Kyle a real ghost would've been far more welcome.

Claudius cleared his throat. "All of this brings me back to my main point. Hammie, with this latest stunt, the only thing you've proven is that you are *not* fit to rule. The laws of the land are very clear. The king must be sound of mind, fair of judgment—and not spend his time playing pranks and making up spooky tales, because managing a kingdom is a full-time job!"

Claudius gestured with his right hand, and two guards approached Hamlet, one on either side. They both held long, very sharp spears.

"I was trying to help you," the king continued, "but it's too late now. I'm going to make a royal proclamation. Sound good? Okay, then," he went on, cutting off Hamlet's reply. "I proclaim that you are no longer a prince, Hammie."

"*Hamlet*," Hamlet spat out, but Claudius wasn't done.

"I also proclaim that you are grounded, forever. You'll be locked in your chambers until further notice. And by 'until further notice,' I mean 'until the sun explodes.' Your personal library will be locked up. The only books you'll be allowed to read will be my own masterpiece, *A Short History of the Eggplant*, volumes one through twenty-seven."

Hamlet's face dropped like someone had just smashed twenty-seven eggplants into it. The guards hefted their spears higher on their shoulders, and their well-polished heads glittered in the torchlight.

"Blinkystick!"

Gross Gabe appeared from under a chair, quickly crawling at one of Claudius's men like a tiny guard dog.

"Shineey! Shineey!"

"What in the—?" Claudius got out. "Guards, remove that pest!"

One of the guards stepped forward, reaching down to grab Gross Gabe with one hand and readying his spear with the other.

"NO!" Kyle yelled, big-brother mode switching on automatically. It felt like he had no control of himself as he did the dumbest thing possible: He ran straight at the guard.

The words poured out of his mouth while his helpless brain sat back and watched it happen. "No! That's my brother, and he's *not allowed near sharp things*!"

Kyle knocked the spear away from Gabe. The guard, shocked, actually dropped it. The sharp end swung down, missed Claudius's nose by inches, and slashed open a large pouch on his belt.

Dozens of little green balls spilled out.

Several of them hit the floor and popped open, unleashing skunkblossom in its most concentrated form. It was like a tidal wave of rotten fruit crashing against a beach covered in week-old whale carcasses.

"The stink bombs!" Halley cried.

But no one could hear her.

They were too busy running, jumping, crawling, and climbing away from the unleashed stench. One lord leaped into a barrel of water. Two ladies grabbed torches and frantically waved them around to clear the air, almost lighting each other on fire.

Chaos reigned.

And it really stank.

CHAPTER SEVENTEEN
CAUGHT ROTTEN-HANDED!

Everyone panicked when the stink bombs hit.
Everyone, that is, except for those with mint
stuffed up their noses, and Claudius, who
whipped a cloth from his pocket and tied it
around his nose and mouth and inhaled deeply.
He'd soaked his handkerchief in some sort of
sickly sweet cologne, and from where Kyle stood
he could smell it even over the stink bombs.

"It was him!" Halley said, pointing to

Claudius. "He made the castle smell bad! He set Hamlet up!"

Unfortunately, nobody was listening.

"You'll never stop me!" Claudius bellowed through the handkerchief on his face. He looked like the Wild West's fanciest cowboy. "Guards!"

He crossed his arms and waited for his guards to seize the four kids. Then he looked left and right and realized the guards were just as nasally distressed as everyone else.

"Drats," he said. "I *knew* I should have given the guards Tybalt's Violent Violet-infused hankies, too."

"The smell is the *least* bad thing you've done since you took over," Ophelia said.

The ladies and lords of the court were starting to succumb to the stink bombs. They began falling to the ground, unable to escape the dreadful fumes.

"We need to clear out the smell and wake them up!" Hamlet said. "They need to see what he really is! And we can't let Claudius escape . . ."

He took a step toward a sleeping duchess, stopped, and then took a step toward Claudius. He looked back and forth, unable to decide what to do first.

Ophelia did not have trouble deciding. She picked up a huge goose drumstick, raised it over her head, and charged at Claudius.

"Come on!" Halley said to Kyle. "She's too small to take him alone!"

Kyle picked up his brother and gave him a tight squeeze. "I missed you, little buddy. I promise I'll always take care of you."

"Iss yoo!" Gabe said happily, and patted
Kyle's hair with his sticky hands. Carefully,
Kyle put Gabe under a chair where he wouldn't
accidentally be hurt. After all that had
happened, he wasn't going to take any chances.

"Oo uck!" Gabe said as Kyle armed himself
with a big handful of grapes. Halley took a
bread stick in each hand. They joined the
chase.

```
It was the first food fight in
the history of the kingdom.
Kyle, Ophelia, and Halley
battled Claudius with food.
They hurled pudding bowls
like grenades and fenced
with asparagus spears,
```

```
forcing Claudius to back up
. . . right into Hamlet,
who was still trying to
decide what to do: wake the
court or chase the king.
```

"Thanks for your help!" Halley said. "Hope you're enjoying all this!"

```
Tremendously. Please, don't
let me interrupt your battle
for the fate of a kingdom.
```

Claudius suddenly grabbed Hamlet in a tight grip and then snatched a butter knife from the table. He held the knife to Hamlet's throat.

"All of you, back!" he shouted, eyes blazing.

Kyle, Ophelia, and Halley screeched to a halt.

"Now then," Claudius said. "Let's discuss the terms of your—your—"

The blood drained from his face and the knife dropped from his hand. "AAAAAAAAAAHHH!"

Kyle followed Claudius's gaze.

There, hovering two feet from the ground and glowing like a lamp, was a ghost.

A *real* ghost.

"See?" cried Hamlet. "I told you so."

CHAPTER EIGHTEEN
GHOST ATTACK!

Kyle screamed!

Halley screamed!

Ophelia and Hamlet screamed!

This was definitely *not* someone wearing a sheet in a wheelbarrow.

It was a ghost.

Even though Kyle could see through the bluish-white specter, its features were very clear.

It was a man about Claudius's age. In fact, he looked kind of like Claudius—but he looked even *more* like Hamlet.

"You're dead," Claudius said, his voice quivering.

"Yes," the ghost said. "It's kind of hard to be a ghost when you're alive. I mean, I never tried it, but it seems like that wouldn't work, right?"

"Dad?" Hamlet gasped.

"Hey, junior," the ghost said, smiling. "Sorry to just drop in like this. I've been trying to get a hold of you for the past week or so, but I think there are some transmission problems. Of course, I was happily slumbering until *somebody* stank up Elsinore so bad that I

couldn't sleep anymore. You think about *that*,
Claudius."

The ghost crossed his arms. "Your stink
bombs smelled so bad, they *woke the dead.*"

"*My* stink bombs?" Claudius said in a quiet
squeak. He cleared his throat. "I—I don't know
what you're talking about."

"Maybe he's talking about that pouch on
your belt full of stink bombs," Hamlet said.

"Not to mention the secret storage room full
of more stink bombs," Kyle said.

The putrid cloud of the stench was finally
clearing out. All around them, the court was
waking up. Some of them looked as though
they thought they were still dreaming while
others gasped with terror.

"Ladies and gentlemen of the court," Hamlet
said to the awakening crowd, "my uncle is

responsible for this grisly smell. Claudius has a storeroom filled with enough ingredients for stink bombs and poison that he could knock everyone out from here to Verona!"

Everyone's eyes turned to Claudius.

"Nonsense!" the king squawked. "The Upper North Wing's been closed for years! There's no secret storeroom there full of snake venom and redcap mushrooms and stolen Montagues' Stinky Mozzarella Pizza Cheese!"

"Hamlet didn't say *where* the room was or *what* was in it," Halley said with a grin. "You've been caught!"

Claudius's mouth flapped slightly, but nothing came out of it.

"I think I've figured out King Claudius's Evil Master Plan," Ophelia said.

Kyle turned to watch Ophelia walk over to a

tray with a goblet on it. The tray had a note that said: *For Hammie.*

"Can I have everyone's attention, please?" Ophelia asked.

But everyone ignored her.

And honestly, Kyle couldn't blame them. It was hard to look at anything else when there was a real-life (or real-dead?) ghost in front of them.

"Hey!" Ophelia said, snapping her fingers. "I'm trying to uncover treason here. Anybody?"

"LOOK AT OPHELIA," the ghost commanded. "Or, uh, face my ghoooostly wraaaath." He waggled his fingers in the air.

Clearly old King Hamlet was still getting used to being a ghost, but it worked. Everyone's eyes instantly snapped to Ophelia.

"Thank you," she said, and adjusted her

cloak. "This drink was going to be delivered to Hamlet's room."

She took the goblet to a potted plant and tossed it in.

In just a few seconds, the big bushy fern turned brown and shriveled up.

The crowd gasped.

"Phew," Ophelia said, waving her hand in front of her nose. "Just as I thought! Deadly Toadbelch. One of the most toxic and worst-smelling poisons there is."

She took a step back from the plant, her face tinged slightly green.

"That's what the stink bombs were for!" she explained. "Claudius filled the castle with skunkblossom stink bombs so no one would notice the smell of the Toadbelch poison when he finally decided to make his move. He then blamed the stinkiness on Hamlet, so that the court would find him too untrustworthy and immature to rule. Once Hamlet was out of the public eye, Claudius could take this final step"—she pointed to the poisoned plant—"to make sure he was never a threat again."

"The same poison he used on me," the ghost said somberly, gazing at the plant. Kyle's jaw dropped. Every time he thought Claudius couldn't get more evil . . .

The crowd gasped. Finally—*finally*—they believed.

"Well, that settles it," Prince Hamlet said, standing up straighter. "I've always wanted to say this . . . *Guards! Get him!*"

The two guards closest to Claudius looked at Hamlet, then nodded.

But before they could grab him, Claudius

shoved the guards aside, spun on his heels, and bolted out the nearest door. Other guards from around the room rushed after him.

"Try the Upper North Wing!" Hamlet shouted after them.

"Shineeey! Shineeey!" Gabe shouted, and pointed toward the crown that had fallen off as Claudius ran for his life.

Ophelia walked up to Gabe. "Good idea, young knight," she said. She picked up Claudius's crown, then took Hamlet's arm. Together they walked to the throne, and Hamlet sat down.

"I crown thee," Ophelia said, placing the crown on Hamlet's head, "*King* Hamlet."

The crowd stared, still unsure.

Then the ghost clapped—and *everyone* instantly broke into applause.

"Long live the king!" the ghost said in a slightly threatening voice.

"Long live the king!" everyone else shouted in a slightly terrified voice.

Kyle raised his arm in the air as he cheered, then immediately pulled it back down as the pain in his bladder came back full force. He still *really* had to go.

The ghost floated up to Hamlet.

"Good work, son," he said. "I'm very proud of you. I wish I could stick around but, you know, I'm deceased."

"Understood, Dad," Hamlet said, smiling. "Feel free to visit anytime."

"I'll be sure to warn you next time," the ghost said, and then he vanished in a thin mist.

"So what do you want to do, Your Highness?" Halley asked with a grin.

"Well," Hamlet said as he settled into the throne, "my first act as king will be to undo every new rule that Claudius made, as of right now. It'll be a lot of work to fix everything, but that's part of being a king. It's not about giving orders and wearing a crown. It's about understanding what your people need. The people of Denmark need justice and fairness. I promise you: People who tell the truth in this kingdom will not be called *liar* or *mad* until there is firm, solid proof that they actually are lying!"

Kyle nodded his approval of Hamlet's kingliness and noticed Halley doing the same. They smiled at each other. Was Halley turning into his *friend*? He wasn't sure if that was more or less weird than Hamlet's ghost father appearing to help them out. Hamlet's talk about justice and fairness made Kyle think that maybe he hadn't given Halley a fair shot. Maybe.

"Furthermore," Hamlet continued, "to honor

the strange guests Kyle, Halley, and Gabe for their help, I declare them all Knights of the Order of, um, let's see . . ." He scratched his head.

"I don't think you'd fit well in any of our knightly orders, so I'll just make a new one. I am king, after all! I hereby decree that you are the first three Knights in the Order of the"—he looked around and his eyes settled on a guard's spear—"the Order of the Spear."

"Shinystick!" Gross Gabe said, crawling up to the throne.

"No spears," Kyle said quickly, hopping from leg to leg. "He's not great with sharp things."

"Order of the Fake Spear, then," said Hamlet, picking up Gross Gabe. "Are there any requests I can grant you?"

"*Yes!*" Kyle shouted. "You can tell me where I can finally pee. *Please.* Your Majesty."

"Go down that hall," Hamlet said, pointing. "There's a latrine right outside."

Quick as a flash, Kyle bolted down the hall . . . and finally found relief.

CHAPTER NINETEEN
THEY ALL LIVED HAPPILY EVER AFTER . . . EXCEPT THE GHOST, WHO WAS NOT ALIVE

When Kyle arrived back in the throne room
(about a gallon lighter), he saw the guards had
returned . . . but without Claudius.

"We searched the castle from attic to cellar,"
one of them said to Hamlet. "He's gone."

"He might be in the secret passages,"
Ophelia said. "We should search there, too."

"Actually," Hamlet said, "why don't we
just put guards at all of the secret passage

entrances? It's not like there's food and water in there. If that's where he is, he won't last long."

The guard nodded, turned, and left. Hamlet's head sagged a little. The big crown almost fell off. "He probably isn't, though. I bet he's long gone from the castle by now."

Unbeknownst to them, Claudius had somehow managed to stumble upon a different, long-forgotten secret passage. A moment of inspiration had led him to it.

"Inspiration," Kyle whispered. "Sure. You helped him escape, didn't you?"

If you wish to lodge a complaint, please contact

the Unsatisfactory Plot
Twist Department.

"Really? You have one of those?"

No.

"It's possible he did get away," Ophelia said. "But what matters is that he's not the king anymore, and people know how terrible he was. If he tries to come back, we'll be ready."

"You have the kingdom's thanks for helping defeat Claudius," Hamlet said. "I have a feeling there are more villains in store for us."

"Oof," Kyle said. "I hope not. Can you take us to the library now? All I want to do is find the Narrator's book and read the end so we can go home."

"I beg your pardon," the ghost said, reappearing from nowhere. Half the people in the room yelped with shock. Kyle, inches away from where he had reappeared, fell flat on his back.

"Oh, um, sorry," the ghost said. "I was just hovering around a bit to make sure Claudius didn't come back. Did I hear you mention the Narrator?"

"Yeah," Kyle said, wobbling back to his feet. "Why? Do you know the Narrator?"

"Nobody does," the ghost said, shaking his head. "But ghosts spend a lot of their time watching the living world and eavesdropping. Word is, the Get Lost Book Club is a permanent membership. Once you're in, you're in. I've heard that you can maybe get off the list if you can find the Narrator, but like I said . . ." He drifted off.

Kyle let out a sigh that felt about a year long. "I'm too tired to figure this out right now. Can you at least help us get home?"

"Yes," the ghost said. "I'll accompany you to the library."

Kyle and Halley shook hands with Hamlet and Ophelia.

"It's been fascinating," Halley said. "I have so much to think about and read. There's a lot of interesting stuff about castles and royalty and everything that I don't know much about."

"True," Kyle admitted, nodding. "As crazy and dangerous as this has been, we've seen a lot of new things. I guess there's more to be found in books than I gave them credit for. All of this throne stealing and graveyards and ghosts was pretty cool."

"And don't forget you saved your brother!"
Halley said. "And helped Hamlet save his
kingdom."

"We both did," Kyle said, and Halley smiled.

"We're so glad that Claudius is gone,"
Ophelia said. "Thank you."

"Visit whenever you like," Hamlet added. "Heroes are always welcome in Denmark."

Kyle's heart sent out a warm pulse. The prince had called him a hero. Maybe he *was* more like Mal and Cal Worthy than he had thought.

"It's been weird," Kyle said. "But, you know, it felt really good to do something important and exciting. If we have to do something like this again"—he glanced at the ghost—"I hope it's also about helping people in danger, and that we meet people as good as you two."

"Safe travels," Hamlet said. Kyle picked up Gabe and followed the ghost out of the throne room.

The main library was bigger and less cramped than Hamlet's private library, although it felt a little colder and less friendly. The ghost led them through towering shelves to a spot near the very back and pointed to a book.

"That one look familiar? I was hiding—I mean, doing important spirit stuff—in here earlier today and it just appeared there."

Kyle handed his spear to Halley and grabbed the thick, leather-bound book. *Hamlet* was in gold on its cover. He ran his hand over the smooth leather. The cover was dull and lifeless on the outside. He never would have expected such a wild world inside.

"Oook! Oook!" Gabe giggled on Kyle's hip.

"This is it," he said.

"Finally," Halley said. "Amazing how much trouble that's caused." She looked around. "It's too bad we can't browse here for a while. I bet there are some great books in this collection."

"Uh, hello? Snake moats and stink bombs?" Kyle said.

Halley smiled. "Don't worry. I want to get out of here right now as quick as we can."

"Good." Kyle riffled through to the back of the book. He cleared his throat. "Ready?"

Halley put her hand on his shoulder. "In case we get separated. I don't want to be left behind."

"Okay, here goes nothing!" Kyle said, and gave Gabe a slight squeeze. He began to read: *"HORATIO: Good night, sweet prince, and flights of angels sing thee to thy rest . . ."*

He tried to read on, but the words blurred— and not the way they usually did in school. The ink *actually* blurred, as though it had been left in the rain too long.

The book shook and twitched, doubling in size in seconds.

Kyle dropped the book to the floor, and it

got even bigger, bigger than he and Halley and Gabe combined.

When it was so big they were in danger of being crushed into the shelves, it opened wide, and a tornado of pages erased the world around them.

CHAPTER TWENTY
THE END?

The fall into Kyle's living room felt like getting
spit out by a giant frog. Kyle wrapped Gabe up in
his arms to cushion him and rolled through the
landing. Letting his brother go, he picked himself
up off the floor and took two dizzy steps.

Kyle blinked.

Then blinked again.

It wasn't until the third blink that he
realized he wasn't seeing things: Becca and

her stepbrother, Sam, had just appeared in the room as well, along with their huge, clumsy dog, Rufus. Not only that, it looked like only a

few minutes had passed here while hours had gone by in Elsinore.

"You made it!" Kyle and Becca said at the same time.

"Where were you?" Sam and Halley asked, also at the same time.

"That was crazy," everyone said together.

"Did you get sucked into a book, too?" asked Becca.

"Yes! Where did your magic trap book take you?" Kyle said.

"Right into the middle of a pizza-based civil war in an Italian town," Becca said. "The unlikeliest love story I've ever seen, between this girl named Juliet and a guy named Romeo. There were tomatoes flying everywhere, and an angry swordsman with terrible cologne, and cheese theft."

"Whoa," Kyle said. He gave Sam and Becca a very quick version of what had happened to them.

"Hey, Roodly Roo!" Halley said as Rufus walked over to her. She bent down to pet his head. "I bet you had a tough time, huh, pups?"

"He'll probably never eat a tomato again," Sam said.

Kyle raised an eyebrow. He didn't like tomatoes, but they were all right on pizza.

"We'll tell you all about it," Sam said. "In fact, we should definitely, absolutely all sit down and go over whatever just happened in more detail so we can figure out what to do next."

Becca tapped Sam on the shoulder, and they had a conversation too quiet for Kyle to hear over Gabe's and Rufus's laughing and yowling as they played together on the floor.

"Do you think what the ghost said was true?" Halley asked Kyle. "About"—she looked around, took a step closer to Kyle, and whispered—"the Narrator."

Kyle flinched, almost expecting a booming echo of *The Narrator, the Narrator, the Narrator* . . . to bounce around the room.

"I don't know," he said. "I don't want to find out. We know how this works now, so we should be able to avoid it."

"Maybe we'd better lock the books up someplace, too," Halley said. "I won't say that wasn't a little exciting, but it's not how I want every Tuesday afternoon to go."

"What do you mean, every Tuesday?" Kyle said.

"Your mom didn't tell you?" Halley said. "The meeting my mom had today is going to be a weekly thing. Maybe for a long time. And my dad's always worked late on Tuesdays, so . . ."

"Tuesday is *Allosaurus, MD* day . . . ," Kyle said. Halley's smile faded, and he quickly finished his sentence. " . . . so I guess I'll just have to record it and watch it on Wednesdays now. You're responsible if I get any spoilers," he said, pointing at her threateningly.

Halley saluted. "I will guard your unspoiledness with all my might. Unless we keep getting eaten by magical books, of course."

Kyle smiled, and they turned back to Sam and Becca.

"First," Becca said, "let's pack these books up and ship 'em back. Or bury them. Something."

She looked around until she saw *Romeo and Juliet* lying on the floor. She reached out a hand very slowly, brushing a corner of the book and then yanking her hand away. When nothing happened, she picked it up.

"Hey," she said, "wait a minute. . . ." She grasped something between her finger and thumb and pulled it out of the book. It was a piece of paper. "Ugh. Anyone else want to read this?"

Kyle shook his head very fast.

"I'll do it," Halley said, and Becca handed her the note.

"*Dear Reader*," Halley read, rolling her eyes. "*I hope you enjoyed your first thrilling and educational expedition with the Get Lost Book Club. No doubt you already miss the escape our club can give you from ordinary life. Don't worry, though. This was just the first of many adventures to come.*"

"Oh no," Kyle said, crossing his arms.

"Absolutely not. No. I'm never opening one of those old books again."

"I don't know if I'll ever open *any* book again," Becca said. "What if I got nabbed by a math textbook or a train schedule?"

"I have some *great* ideas for future *Mal & Cal Worthy* adventures, though," Kyle said to Becca.

"Me, too!" she replied. "If we don't win the Storyland contest this year, we'll definitely win it next year. But let's talk about that after we've hurled these books into the sun."

"Yeah," Kyle agreed. "I mean, I still want to go to Hawaii eventually, but *Hamlet* was pretty exciting even though I didn't leave my living room. Not"—he quickly added—"that I ever want to get lost in a book again!"

"I hope you've all been having a good time,"

Mom said, walking into the living room with cinnamon-stained hands. She turned her head and saw the book lying at Kyle's feet. "Wow, Kyle, is that *Hamlet*?" she said. "I didn't realize you were studying Shakespeare. You like it?"

Kyle and Halley locked eyes. He tried to ungrit his teeth.

"Yeah," Kyle said. "It was gripping."

"Captivating," Halley said.

"One of those stories you feel like you're right in the middle of," Becca said.

"You can almost smell it," Sam said.

Mom smiled delightedly. "You three are all welcome to stay for dinner if you'd like. Mr. W. said it'll be ready soon. He's got a big pot of tomato soup bubbling."

"Erch," Gabe said. "Wan snacksta-peez!"

"Tomatoes aren't so bad, Gabe," Kyle cut in hurriedly. He'd promised his brother he'd take care of him, and that wouldn't change just because they were out of the book. "They'll make you grow big and strong—like me!"

"Yum?" Gabe asked.

"Yum," Kyle confirmed. "Especially on things like sandwiches and pizza . . ."

"Uh," Sam said, looking slightly green in the face as he grabbed his basketball off the carpet, "I'd love to, but I have to . . . write that essay about, um, carpentry."

He began to back away. "Becca, you need that library book returned, right? I'll grab that and run over to the library first. I bid thee—I mean, have a good night!" He made his exit as if he were being pursued by a bear.

"More for the rest of you," Mom said, smiling. "It should be almost ready—" She suddenly stopped talking and blinked once. "What's that awful smell?"

DEAR READER,

Well done! You've made it to the end with Kyle and Halley, who faced great peril and came out victorious. You helped topple a sinister tyrant, discovered the secret of a haunted castle, and let the people of Elsinore finally unclamp their noses.

Still, questions remain. What *did* happen to Sam and Becca? Who is this strange Italian boy who needs so much help with his poetry? Where did Hamlet's prince crown go?

As with so many things, you can find those answers in a book.

Shakespeare wrote many plays besides *Hamlet*. One in particular, *Romeo and Juliet*, may have some of the answers you need. It also has feuding families, clever sword fighters, and a lot of pizza.

Like countless people before them, Kyle and Halley got lost in a book. And just like so many, they came to the end knowing more, thinking differently, and understanding each other—and themselves—a little better.

Because sometimes the only way to find something new is to get lost.

Until next time,

The Narrator

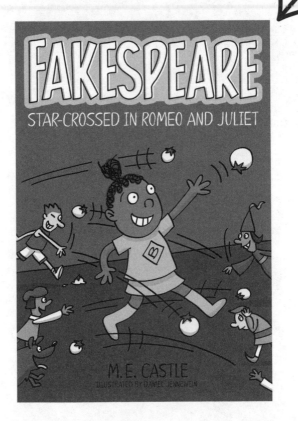

Do you have an eye for epic quests?
Enjoy spending time in your imagination?
Want to go on an adventure?

Then sign up for

STORYLAND YOUNG STORYTELLER CONTEST**

Enter your

SHORT STORY	NOVELLA
POEM	NOVEL
COMIC BOOK	EPIC

and win an

ALL-EXPENSES-PAID TRIP TO OUR HAWAIIAN LOCATION!

For more information, register online, and you'll receive the Storyland Young Storyteller Contest Guidelines in the mail.*

*By participating in the contest, entrant warrants and represents that his/her entry is original to the entrant, has not been previously published or won any award, and does not contain any material that would violate or infringe upon the rights of any third party, including copyrights (including, without limitation, copyrighted images or footage), trademarks, or rights of privacy or publicity.

Please note that by entering the contest, you are also signing up for the Get Lost Book Club, founded by the most wonderful and splendid Narrator of all time.

**Sorry, kids; the Narrator is a jerk, and this contest is not real. He would still like to read your stories, though. Please send them, along with any complaints about his treachery, to the address located in this book—if you can find it (Hint: it's on the copyright page, near a certain book curse).

ABOUT THE AUTHOR

M.E. CASTLE is a New York City-raised writer and actor living in Washington, DC. He is the author of the beloved Clone Chronicles, which introduced the world to Fisher Bas, his clones, a flying pig, and a large supporting cast of robots, aliens, and a very proper talking toaster. When not writing, he can be found performing the works of Shakespeare onstage, which has given him the expertise necessary to create this utterly scholarly and serious work.

ABOUT THE ILLUSTRATOR

DANIEL JENNEWEIN has been drawing since kindergarten, where he could mainly be found drawing skulls and hooks, to the irritation of some adults. He works as a freelance illustrator and art director in Frankfurt. His picture books include *Is Your Buffalo Ready for Kindergarten?* (written by Audrey Vernick, 2010), *Teach Your Buffalo to Play Drums* (written by Audrey Vernick, 2011), and *Chick-o-Saurus Rex* (written by Lenore Jennewein, 2013).

danieljennewein.com

ACKNOWLEDGMENTS

I have been fortunate enough in my life to not only write goofy, whimsical books as a job but to perform Shakespeare live on stage as a job as well. Of all my enthusiastically geeky interests, Shakespeare is hard to top. Stepping into a playing space and embodying characters from and for all time, speaking words committed to paper when the printing press was scarcely more than a century old and reigned as the cutting edge of idea dissemination, is an experience profound and thrilling enough that I couldn't possibly give this sentence an ending that would do it justice.

It was that deep fondness in my heart that led to these books, and the odd adventures of the characters within. They aren't severe departures from Shakespearean tendencies, either. His plays *are* full of silly jokes and "lowbrow" humor. They *are*, for the most part, straightforward stories with big, easily relatable themes. And they *are* entirely capable of being appreciated—and understood—by young audiences. It's my hope that the Fakespeare tales will be enjoyed both as stories in their own right and as a way to tell young readers not to be afraid of Shakespeare.

I must thank the excellent people at Paper Lantern, in particular Kamilla Benko and Lexa Hillyer, the latter of whom helped with this project while preparing to have and subsequently caring for an entirely other tiny human, a task I can't conceive the dauntingness of. I also extend heartfelt thanks to the good people at Macmillan, without whom you could read this book only if I printed it out, walked up, and handed it to you. My editor (and publisher of Imprint)

Erin Stein, editorial assistant Nicole Otto, creative director

Natalie C. Sousa, associate marketing director Kathryn

Little, publicist Kelsey Marrujo, senior production manager

Raymond Ernesto Colón, and production editor Ilana Worrell.

I also want to thank those who led me down the path

to Shakespeare: Woody Howard, one of my first acting

teachers and the subject of this book's dedication, and

Paul Moser, whose Shakespeare acting course was the

centerpiece of my acting training. I also want to toss

some thanks to the good people of the Adirondack

Shakespeare Company who keep hiring me to act in

their productions even after getting to know me.

As always, thanks to all of my friends for giving me

someone to discuss these cool things with, my mother and

sister for taking time out of doing great things themselves

to cheer me on, and a lady named Andrea whom I asked

to dance a few years ago and, to my great fortune, haven't

yet trod on the toes of enough to end that dance.